THE LEGACY SERIES

SERIES TITLES

We Should Be Somewhere by Now
Stephen Tuttle

Burner and Other Stories
Katrina Denza

The Plan of Chicago
Barry Pearce

The Caged Man
Calvin Mills

A Day Doesn't Go By When I Don't Have Regrets
J. Malcolm Garcia

These Are My People
Steve Fox

Trust Issues
K.P. Davis

Adult Children
Laurence Klavan

Guardians & Saints
Diane Josefowicz

Western Terminus: Stories and A Novella
Michael Keefe

Like Human
Janet Goldberg

The Hopefuls
Elizabeth Oness

Never Stop Exiting
Michael Hopkins

Broken Heart Syndrome
Anne Colwell

The Mexican Messiah: A Novella & Stories
Jay Kauffmann

Close to a Flame
Colleen Alles

American Animism
Jamey Gallagher

Keeping What's Best Left Kept Secret
David Ricchiute

Soaked
Toby LeBlanc

The Path of Totality
Marie Zhuikov

Shocker in Gloomtown
Dan Libman

The Continental Divide
Bob Johnson

The Three Devils and Other Stories
William Luvaas

The Correct Response
Manfred Gabriel

Welcome Back to the World: A Novella & Stories
Rob Davidson

Greyhound Cowboy and Other Stories
Ken Post

Close Call
Kim Suhr

The Waterman
Gary Schanbacher

Signs of the Imminent Apocalypse and Other Stories
Heidi Bell

What We Might Become
Sara Reish Desmond

The Silver State Stories
Michael Darcher

An Instinct for Movement
Michael Mattes

The Machine We Trust
Tim Conrad

Gridlock
Brett Biebel

Salt Folk
Ryan Habermeyer

The Commission of Inquiry
Patrick Nevins

Maximum Speed
Kevin Clouther

Reach Her in This Light
Jane Curtis

The Spirit in My Shoes
John Michael Cummings

*The Effects of Urban Renewal on Mid-Century America and
Other Crime Stories*
Jeff Esterholm

What Makes You Think You're Supposed to Feel Better
Jody Hobbs Hesler

Fugitive Daydreams
Leah McCormack

Hoist House: A Novella & Stories
Jenny Robertson

Finding the Bones: Stories & A Novella
Nikki Kallio

Self-Defense
Corey Mertes

Where Are Your People From?
James B. De Monte

Sometimes Creek
Steve Fox

The Plagues
Joe Baumann

The Clayfields
Elise Gregory

Kind of Blue
Christopher Chambers

Evangelina Everyday
Dawn Burns

Township
Jamie Lyn Smith

Responsible Adults
Patricia Ann McNair

Great Escapes from Detroit
Joseph O'Malley

Nothing to Lose
Kim Suhr

The Appointed Hour
Susanne Davis

"Playful, poignant, and profound, these dazzling fictions shimmer in the jittery spaces between eloquent parable and sharp-edged realism, anxious absurdism and potent allegory. Mysteries abound: your wife shrinks so thin she almost vanishes; bees colonize your home; your neighbor builds a cage bigger than a house and slight as a shadow—a cage for other cages, a trap of wire with no interior. In these uncanny worlds, haunted by inexplicable disappearances and unspoken grief, anything can happen. Stephen Tuttle ferries us to the far shore of sorrow with humor and grace, tenderly exposing the quiet terrors that flood our hearts in the borderlands between sleep and death."

—MELANIE RAE THON
author of *Sweet Hearts*

WE SHOULD BE SOMEWHERE BY NOW

stories

Stephen Tuttle

CORNERSTONE PRESS

UNIVERSITY OF WISCONSIN-STEVENS POINT

Cornerstone Press, Stevens Point, Wisconsin 54481
Copyright © 2025 Stephen Tuttle
www.uwsp.edu/cornerstone

Printed in the United States of America by
Point Print and Design Studio, Stevens Point, Wisconsin

Library of Congress Control Number: 2025944933
ISBN: 978-1-968148-13-3

This is a work of fiction. Names, characters, businesses, places, events, and incidents
are either the products of the author's imagination or used in a fictitious manner. Any
resemblance to actual persons, living or dead, or actual events is purely coincidental.

Cornerstone Press titles are produced in courses and internships offered by the
Department of English at the University of Wisconsin–Stevens Point.

DIRECTOR & PUBLISHER
Dr. Ross K. Tangedal

EXECUTIVE EDITORS
Jeff Snowbarger, Freesia McKee

EDITORIAL DIRECTOR
Brett Hill

SENIOR EDITORS
Paige Biever, Eva Nielsen, Reilly Crous

PRESS STAFF
Karlie Harpold, Lilly Kulbeck, Brianna Loving, Leo Poskozim, Alex Diaz, Josh
Paulson, Samantha Bjork, Sophie McPherson, Madison Schultz, Autumn Vine

stories

Amanuensis   1

Keepers of Bees   17

Rosenvall's Cage   31

Age, Epoch, Era, Eon   41

The Trees in North America   47

The Future King   64

At the Gates of the Kingdom   75

The Two Mr. Greens   91

The Scold   104

Blight   108

The Tree of the Holy Virgin   124

The Hidden Curriculum   130

In California   138

The Weather Here   148

Maybe the Kids Maybe   156

Undone by the Moon   168

The Funambulist   175

Aboard Abroad   183

Acknowledgments 191

*There was talk about the weather; they congratulated them-
selves on its mildness.*

    —Bernard Malamud, *A New Life*

Amanuensis

1

*L*ater, *when the storms had stopped,* they began to discover what so much snow could do. They saw how it collapsed roofs and bridges and trees. How it made roads impassable and telephones useless. They saw that wild animals, deer and raccoons and foxes, had been forced to look for food at lower and lower elevations until the hunt brought them to the streets of their town, where they found no better luck. For days after, they found carcasses all through their streets: gaunt and empty and wasted. If there were many among them who saw so much snow as a sign from heaven, there were none who called it a blessing. It was a trial or a purification or a mystery, but they couldn't say they were grateful. No one said anything about the drought they wouldn't have to worry over. No one said anything about the reservoir that would reach capacity for the first time in a decade.

Twenty-six consecutive days of heavy snow, one storm beginning before the last one ended, one storm overwhelming another. Nearly a month of constant blizzards, during which they were trapped inside their homes. During those weeks, their churches were empty, their schools locked tight. When it was over, they came out of their homes as though for the first time in their lives. The clouds thinned and the sun shone down and began the weeks-long process of condensing so many feet of snow, compressing it into mounds of hard ice veined with oil and soot. It was then, having come out to inspect the damage, to see what had broken, what had burst, what had failed to endure, that word of Dumond began to circulate. He was one of their neighbors, a junior high school science teacher. He had disappeared into the snow and hadn't returned.

What they heard was that a day or two earlier, when the last storm had begun to fade and another had not come to replace it, Dumond left early in the morning, on foot, intending to photograph ice crystals and falling flakes. This was a hobby of his and it came as no surprise that he would head to the foothills on a day when anyone else would have stayed inside their warm house. Dumond's wife waited through most of the day, she said, before she decided she had waited long enough. Her husband tended to lose time, she knew, but the snow had continued to fall that whole day. If it was tapering off, it was still immense and still fell so heavily at noon that she regretted his decision to leave. She was left to suspect that he had gotten himself stuck in a snowdrift or worse.

They admired Dumond and respected him. Those children who sat through earth science all called him a favorite teacher. His close neighbors called him a credit to society. They wasted no time organizing themselves. They used every means to find and rescue a man who had thought, just prematurely, that the weeks of snow had finally come to an end. If they worked swiftly—after an initial search revealed nothing—they didn't truly hope for success. A day turned into a week. After so many storms had buried them under, they couldn't hope they were going to find him, not in so much snow, not for months. If they were slow to say so, each of them knew that no one could survive an entire week in such conditions.

They asked his wife if it would be all right for them to honor her husband, knowing that she was unlikely to abandon hope, even if it was clear that he was gone for good. This was for the best, for her and for everyone. They took her silence as permission, making the arrangements because there was no family to do it for her. They gathered in a chapel, took turns telling each other just how much they respected this man, just how much his absence would be felt. When they talked about him, they nodded in the direction of a small photograph in a silver frame.

The Dumond family had been a part of this town for as long as anyone could remember. The schools here were rarely without a Mr. or Mrs. Dumond, and neither were various boards and civic committees. A Dumond had been the mayor once, one had been postmaster, and no less than four had stood in front of them on Sunday mornings, preaching again what they had heard so many times before. After so many Dumonds, this was the last. Over the previous decades the family had dwindled: no children replaced those that grew old and passed. Dumond's parents were both dead, killed years earlier and in the same instant, when their car and another collided on a mountain road just minutes from their home. His two brothers were dead, as well: one to heart disease, one to cancer. Neighbors had watched as the Dumond family, this constant presence in their town, reduced itself to this couple. They had had no children of their own and they politely ignored every hint that it wasn't too late to remedy that fact. They stayed to themselves more often than not. Even before the snow, neighbors noticed that these Dumonds, these last Dumonds, weren't as neighborly as they might have been, not as likely to visit over a fence. They rarely saw him outside of school, and they hardly saw her anywhere. They regretted the distance that had grown between them and this family, how they had said nothing, years earlier, when they quietly disappeared from their Sunday congregation.

Former students who attended the memorial were quick to announce their fondness for a man who made science fun. He had taught them so much without making a minute of it seem like work. As a kind of excuse for his final hours, they talked about how much he loved the snow. They recalled their fondness for winter's first storm, how it meant that Mr. Dumond would cancel whatever he had scheduled, even a test, to take them outside to examine those early flakes. They recalled the things he taught them about snow crystals, how the popular wisdom about their inexhaustible variation was true but that there was more to the story. He told them that each snowfall contained millions of crystals that were nearly identical to each other and that any distinction was not a matter of creation but of environment, that each was formed minutes or hours earlier, far above the earth, and that these crystals collided and joined and broke apart in the air, that what they saw in their hands, falling onto their tongues, captured on sheets of glass to be viewed under a microscope, were indicators of atmospheric conditions. The infinite patterns were there, but did they notice the consistency of their shape, the perfect hexagonal symmetry of each flake? These were the result of a specific wind speed and humidity and temperature. He showed them photographs of snowflakes he had taken, photographs they could hardly believe were of naturally occurring phenomena. The complexity was incredible, the balance surprising. They couldn't see the world the same way after Mr. Dumond taught them to look at snow. They were indebted to him forever.

2

It was late spring, the snow melted and gone, when children—playing where they had been told not to—first learned that the empty Dumond house was not empty at all. Already bored with their own backyards and the quiet routine of empty fields, the children examined the locked doors and windows of the house until something gave under pressure and allowed them inside. Dumond's wife had left without a goodbye. She had hired a moving company and was gone before anyone had the chance to offer help. Neighbors told their children to stay away from that house, that it wasn't theirs to creep around in, and that sooner or later someone would buy it and fix it up. They also suspected that the house might never sell, that it might sit there empty for years, surrounded by its weeds. If they didn't show it—to maintain consistency, to appear disappointed by a rule not obeyed—the parents of those children were delighted to know that someone, finally, had explored the space where the Dumonds once lived. What their children told them, when they sheepishly reported what they had done, was that in the basement of the Dumond house they had found an entire city.

Where they expected to find nothing more than empty rooms, their children had found a series of tables filling the vast middle of Dumond's basement, and on those tables were miniature churches and miniature stores and miniature houses in cul-de-sacs. When those parents and other neighbors finally came to inspect that basement, they saw that this was not just a toy model of some generic town, not just some three-dimensional, plastic landscape on which children might arrange toy cars, but a perfect replica of their town with their hardware store, their bakery, and their supermarket. For what it was, it was larger than anything they had ever seen. No map, no model, no miniature they had known had been so enormous in its scope and so precise in its detail. They stood there amazed, admiring the size of their town and how large it seemed now that it was so small. How it stretched out around the low hills surrounding them, how it filled the long space of its valley. They stood in awe of Dumond's scale model.

There was a swell of pride in those first encounters with the model town, a sense of confidence that this place merited a scale replica, as though it were the site of a civil war battle or an example of visionary city planning. Neighbors and citizens, former students and their parents, everyone came to the empty house. They came to see the model and they came to see how accurately it was built, to see which details were included and which were not. They found the movie theater and the dry cleaners, the auto body shop and the sporting goods. They found the library and its statue garden, the cemetery and the vast, open park behind it. They even found the model train shop, a scale model of a store that sold scale models. They applauded Dumond for his attention to detail, they clapped their hands and smiled, impressed by the painstaking hours he must have dedicated to this work.

It was only later, when they were returning for a fourth or fifth visit, that they began to notice small mistakes that hadn't caught their eyes before. If Dumond had given each house its correct number, the paint he had chosen for a given door was often the wrong color. The headstones in the cemetery were blank. The marquee above the movie theater looked right, but the jumble of letters there said nothing at all. The wide variety of trees that lined their streets and filled their yards (elms and maples, willows and oaks) were represented by a largely scattershot arrangement of a single tree, a dummy version of some generic thing that corresponded to nothing they had ever seen. The precision that had impressed them at first was only a broad and general accuracy. The close detail they had seen was never truly there. This map was not the impressive reproduction they had taken it for. It was large, of course, and clearly the result of long work. But still, they had taken it for something greater, something immense and impossible. They tried to remind themselves that they had never created anything close to this themselves. They reminded themselves that no map is as precise as the one you hope for.

What bothered them more were the markings they found all over this miniature town of theirs. There, among this reproduction of their landscape, was a network of colored dots placed inexplicably on the corner of a roof or a window. They hadn't noticed them at first, but now they could see little more than the markings that filled the map, markings that corresponded to nothing they knew of. There were colored dots and nearly invisible numbers and letters, filled shapes and empty shapes, and dozens of icons they couldn't identify at all. Some of the markings they could guess at. They could tell, for example, that the various colored lines that ran along their streets, corresponded in some way to their traffic patterns: a busy street was nearly filled, while the streets they lived on, and especially the dead ends, were almost empty. Their homes were also covered in markings, laid out in such a way that they appeared to be embellishments at first, as though this series of symbols might have been an architectural flourish, some contemporary design. They began to document the marks on their homes and compare them as though they were Boy Scout merit badges or baseball cards they had collected. They attempted to translate Dumond's cryptic language, identifying which of them shared a red dot, which had the symbol of an opened eye, who had three yellow slashes and who had two overlapping circles.

By the time they discovered the key to Dumond's symbols they had already invented one of their own. They had decided that certain markings were desirable and that others were not. They had begun to clap each other on the back when two houses shared a mark, when two neighborhoods on either side of the model town were found to match. They had determined that the markings were indications of certain verifiable facts: who drove which cars, who worked which jobs, whose property value had increased the most in recent years. They were right in their first general assumptions about the markings, but wrong in nearly every particular. It was a substitute teacher at Dumond's school who finally stumbled upon the key, filed away in the back of a cabinet the substitute had never felt was hers to use. After so many months, she finally decided to discard the things Dumond was not around to need. The key itself was hand-written and covered in smudges and corrections, originally typed but layered now in ink from a dozen pens. It was ten pages of symbols and their translations.

The key made the map seem innocuous at first. They had been right about the markings of traffic and walking routes, and right that certain markings indicated water and power lines, and right that other markings indicated the value of real estate. But they couldn't have guessed at most of Dumond's symbols. He had markings to indicate their faith and the regularity of their attendance at church, how much debt they carried, what politics they endorsed, what bias they felt. His map showed things he would have had to watch them to know, and things he shouldn't have known even if he had. He had charted out their lives in the most intrusive ways. He knew the secret routes their children took to school. He knew how much time their teenage daughters spent on the telephone. He knew which houses had the most valuable heirlooms. He knew which of them had trouble sleeping, which used medications for sexual dysfunction, which had been unfaithful to a spouse. They knew, almost immediately, that Dumond's information was invented, that it was faulty. He couldn't have known about attempts to defraud insurance companies. He shouldn't have known just how many of their children were left unattended in the late afternoon when any stranger might walk right in and have his way.

If they denied each revelation Dumond's map seemed to make of them, they were also eager to spend more time in his old basement. They said very little to each other about what they saw there, except to scoff at a ridiculous hobby. They were quick to forget the praise they had had for Dumond. They were quick to recall just how much they had always disliked him.

3

They often forgot that Dumond's wife was named Kathleen. They called her Catherine, Kelly, Karen, Carolyn and even when they stumbled upon the right name, they were never confident that they had found it. They attempted her name without conviction because many of them had not met her, and many more had never seen her. She was foreign to them the way a distant relative might be, she was someone who had lived on the periphery of their lives. They knew she was often sick, but the severity of her illnesses ranged, in their many accounts, from a series of colds and allergies to rare viruses and incurable diseases. She was anemic, frail, and on her deathbed, they said. She got migraines and bloody noses, they said. They knew, somehow, that she often slept sixteen hours a day, couldn't stand direct exposure to the sun, and had no capacity for digesting certain common foods.

They knew next to nothing about Kathleen Dumond. They were unable to admit that they had embraced accounts of her illness because they had wanted some excuse for the distance she kept. The people of this town were close to each other, knew each other well, and the fact that Dumond married a woman so unwilling to share in their closeness was something that needed explaining. If they were prepared to believe any account of frailty, they did so out of that kindness they couldn't escape. No one in this town stayed away from the community of it unless they were compelled to. In this way, they talked about this woman, got her name wrong, refused to admit how unlikely their stories were, and prepared a set of excuses for the disappointment they felt.

What they never said, what seemed beyond saying, was that Dumond's wife was inferior to them, came from weaker stock, was less well prepared for living than they were. The people of this town didn't get sick, didn't stay in their houses when the sun was out and work needed doing, didn't like to think about the various ways a human body might fail. They were strong and set about their lives with a sense of earned confidence. Dumond's wife, on the other hand, was a transplant and had come here only after Dumond had gone away to college, returning, half a dozen years later, new wife in tow. They talked about what might have motivated him, why Dumond should have chosen to look elsewhere for what was clearly to be found among them. Still, they were forced to admit that, for as little as they knew about his wife, they didn't know all that much about Dumond, either. They knew that their children couldn't stop talking about this favorite teacher, but wasn't he the same man who didn't enjoy his hometown enough to truly be part of it? Wasn't he the same man who traveled every summer, who disappeared for months at a time and never thought to explain his absence?

Their children seemed to know the Dumonds had been around the world, that they had seen the Pyramids, the Great Wall, and the Leaning Tower. They seemed to know that Dumond and his wife saved and saved on his meager salary so the two of them could travel. Their children were jealous, they said. They regretted the things they hadn't seen, but parents and teachers were quick to remind the children that there was more to the world than sightseeing. They recalled the many virtues of this place, of the camaraderie they felt, of the things you could learn right here, in this town, in these streets, in that garden. They reminded the children that life was richer and more rewarding when one invested oneself in a place, in a community, and that globetrotting was simply a means of dodging responsibility. They said that Dumond might have filled the classroom with fun and games, but he was a mercenary who saw those hours as nothing more than a means to an end.

Some were not as quick to begrudge the Dumonds their travels, but they suspected, and had suspected all along, that Dumond's map was only accurate insofar as it was autobiographical. They argued that the map was an indication that a pervert had lived among them, that they were fortunate to be rid of that influence. They argued that they all ought to be counting blessings in the absence of the Dumonds, that a wicked influence was gone from among them. They argued that God had protected them from an evil they had been blind to, and that they ought to sing praises for that. Did they need more evidence than Dumond's conspicuous absence from their Sunday services? Did they have to look any further than his carnal behavior to see that he was wrong in the head and certainly an influence toward all that is misguided? Some were slower to condemn. They asked everyone to recall that the Dumonds had always been churchgoers, but that they had chosen a different church, a different congregation. They had seen them, hadn't they, entering a small chapel on the edge of town? Hadn't they once heard Dumond say something about marital unity and not wanting to make waves?

All through that summer, at any hour, there was hardly room to stand in Dumond's basement. Neighbors filled that space and shouted at each other about what should be done. Self-appointed guards stood watch over the long series of tables to protect the map from vandalism and destruction. They said that no one was going to touch the model until everyone agreed what they should do, that if it were to be dismantled, they would do it systematically. They said that it needed to be protected from those who would destroy what they couldn't understand. Others set to work transcribing the map, making detailed copies of Dumond's markings. They took photographs and argued that this thing was the work of a preservationist, that it froze time and could be thought of as a historical document. They said it was impressive to think that such an artifact could so enliven a community, could so effectively hold a mirror to a people. This was wrong, they said. They asked if they were expected to believe, as the map suggested, that their neighbors cared so little for their children, or that they were surrounded by the depressed, the destitute, the immoral. This map, they said, was filled with lies. This map was the product of a stranger and a skeptic. He was a scientist, they said, but not a good one. After all, he landed no better than a job at a junior high school in a district notorious for low standards. Some agreed that Dumond had hardly reached the heights of his profession, others said they were appalled to hear such criticism of themselves, the teachers who ate lunch next to Dumond, those who felt owed a certain respect, they said, for choosing to teach in a place like this.

There were those who found themselves conflicted. They were impressed by what Dumond had done, impressed by the stir he had caused, but also suspicious of his facts. They believed that this map was a rudimentary attempt, that it represented a first, broad sketch of this town. If the details were wrong, the idea was right. They said that perhaps the map should be used as a template, but that they should feel free to make corrections and alterations to fit what they knew to be true. They argued that the map could be useful but that it could also do them harm and they needed to be careful. They said that no one could deny that Dumond had hit a nerve and that they would be wrong to simply ignore the significance of his act. This was an opportunity to understand their community better than they had, and they would be foolish not to take it.

One man got a black eye when he said to another that people like Dumond didn't belong in this town. A second man had asked what kind of person the first man thought Dumond was and if this had anything to do with politics. The first man said it was obvious what he meant, and the second man took that as his cue. A woman admitted that she couldn't speak for the rest of her neighbors but that she could verify that Dumond got everything right about her house. She wasn't proud to admit it, she said, but facts were facts. Another woman said that one of two things was true and either Dumond was a regrettable human being or her husband had some explaining to do. Several parents said that they had altered their schedules because of what the map had shown. They believed the map had been wrong, they said, but now they were sure of it. One man said that he would not allow himself to be slandered by the speculations of a dead man. The map may have been right in some few generalities, but it was filled with lies all the same. He had daughters to think of, he had a wife, and he wasn't going to rest easy while that map said what it did about him. Many of them apologized for wrongs they had committed, and others forgave sins that had never been confessed. Still, others refused to let their children play with the sons and daughters of neighbors who had once been close friends.

4

They decided to protect themselves from the map and prohibit anyone from entering the empty house. They locked the doors and windows and said they would give the keys over to the new owners, if anyone ever decided to buy the place. If the house sat there in its vacancy, if it became inaccessible to them, it still occupied much of their thinking and most of their conversations. They recalled what they had seen, arguing over details. They disputed what markings had been on what properties and what the key had revealed. They fought among themselves until many of them refused to speak to one another. They returned to their homes and their lives and said that time would tell, that eventually the basement would be opened and then they'd see who was right.

Some of them talked about opening Dumond's house and fixing the map, adding to the work they saw as incomplete. They would repaint the doors to match the real colors of their real houses, they would find model trees that more accurately represented their real trees, they would paint small human figures and fill the map with the people Dumond had forgotten to include. Their most important addition would be no addition at all. They would remove every marking that didn't correspond to something they could see with their own eyes. They would destroy the key and clear the model town of the symbols that had so bothered and confused them. It would be better, they said. The map was a beautiful thing that anyone but a fool would admire. They would reinforce the tables Dumond had worked on and place a velvet rope around them. They would have electricians install a series of ceiling lights to best allow inspection of each wonderful detail. For years they could come and be impressed by the map. They argued for intervention, saying that the map would erode with time, that they needed to keep it free of dust. They said it would take years, but that eventually the map would show signs of age, that it would fail. If they could look after it, however, if they could care for it, they could save it.

Some of them claimed to have seen Dumond wandering in the darkness of their homes and backyards. Some said they saw him watching from a distance through binoculars. He wasn't dead at all, they said, and he wasn't gone. If he had disappeared into the snow, he had only gone into hiding. They recalled the body they never found, the wife who disappeared in the night. They talked about the model town and how it infected them.

Some considered dismantling the map and hiding it away. They might gently separate it into parts and scatter the pieces throughout town. They might take each miniature church and lock it in a cabinet of a real church. They might take the miniature model of their movie theatre and hide it in the projection booth. They might slide the models of their homes beneath their beds in the bedrooms. They might spread the map to the far extremes of what it represented, hiding each part as close as possible to the thing it was meant to be. They told themselves this would be a way to remember, and that later, when they felt comfortable reconstructing the map, they would have little trouble finding its constituent parts. They knew that by exploding this map they could save it, that they could make it real. Dumond's map would be safe, they knew, if they could bury it inside their town, every piece where it needed to be.

Then, after the long heat of August was gone and the leaves had begun to turn, some of them destroyed Dumond's scale model. They overwhelmed those who would have kept it and protected it. They tore it apart and crushed it, smashing it onto the concrete floor of that basement. They ran from the house carrying large sections of the map, dragging behind them long sheets of plastic and pieces of green felt. They soaked everything in gasoline and watched it burn in the middle of the street. They tore the key to Dumond's map into shreds and then burned the shreds. They congratulated themselves on a work completed, on an evil banished. They smiled and said that now, at least, they could relax, knowing that nothing of Dumond was left among them. They wouldn't make eye contact with those who had fought so hard to stop them. They wouldn't speak to those who had opposed their plans.

Eventually, their conversations returned to the old things: a football game the previous weekend, a problem at work, a storm in the forecast. They rarely said anything about the long months during which they had grown so distant and angry. If they mentioned Dumond from time to time, it was only the name of a man who once lived here: a good man from a good family they were sad to have lost. They remembered the garden he kept. They remembered how their children had loved his class. They remembered his peculiar hobby: taking photographs of the snow.

When the first storm came, they watched it from behind the windows of their homes. Snow slowly piled on their lawns and sidewalks and streets. The branches of their trees bowed beneath the weight. They marveled, as they had so many times before, at how quiet the world becomes when it's new with snow.

Keepers of Bees

My wife wanted bees.

Bees? I said.

She wanted one of those hives people sometimes have in their yards, the ones that look like little chests of drawers. They come in all shapes and sizes, she said, some decorative and some quite plain. She said she would be more than happy with a plain one.

I explained that the box wasn't my concern. What I really wanted to say was that while the shape and size of the box was something I could be indifferent to, the bees themselves gave me pause. But she took my preface as agreement and said she was glad I felt that way because she'd given the bees a lot of thought and really had her heart set on getting some.

I'll order a colony, she said.

We were sitting on the patio of our favorite restaurant a day or two later. It was one of those summer evenings when the sun seems to pause as it's setting. It was hot, but not too hot, and I was enjoying something called fiesta chicken. My wife had ordered a salad. As we ate, a bee began to hover around the table, buzzing its way from point to point. The bee had taken a liking to me, and I shooed it away several times before it discovered my plate, which it liked even more. It kept landing on the edge before I sent it away with a wave of my hand.

This little guy is driving me crazy, I said, trying to sound unbothered.

My wife didn't say anything at first. She just stared in my direction, lost in thought. I began to eat a little faster, knowing the meat was clearly a draw and knowing that if the bee actually touched my food there was no way I would finish it.

I spent the next few minutes politely fending off the bee until my wife said, It comes tomorrow.

What does?

The colony.

What do you mean? I said. It comes how?

It comes in the mail, she said. Oh, it's so cool. We'll get this whole kit. It's a box with about three pounds of bees. Different sorts, you know.

Three pounds? I said. They sell bees by weight?

She told me they did. When I asked about weighing a bee, I said I thought it was funny to imagine a beekeeper with a little scale, lining up bees like prize fighters before a bout.

My wife didn't think this was funny. She didn't laugh, at least.

How many bees does it take to get to three pounds? I said.

About 10,000.

10,000? I said, sounding, perhaps, a bit hysterical.

Don't worry. The queen will start laying eggs right away. Come spring, we could have ten times that many.

Ten times 10,000?

Yes, she said, almost squealing.

And I suppose each one will want some of my chicken, I said.

I'm sorry? she asked.

As we were standing to leave, I saw that the bee had finally landed on the center of my plate and was marching around like it owned the place.

That night, as we were lying in bed, my wife wanted to say more about bees. She talked about the box and its panels, some of which were already filled with a sugary substance that the bees could feed on as they got started. She said the queen would come in this small cage, surrounded by sugar or wax and that this was to protect her. The worker bees would eat the wax away and set her loose, but not before they had a chance to learn her smell, or something along those lines. She said we wouldn't see honey right away, but that we'd have plenty before long, and that the flowers and fruit trees were going to love this. She was already thinking about other places in the yard where we could set up more boxes.

Are you worried about the children? I said.

What children?

Any children. Neighborhood children. Bees sting kids, you know.

You're thinking of wasps, she said.

I think I'm thinking of bees.

What she meant, she said, was that I must have been thinking of wasps or hornets or yellowjackets if I meant to suggest that random children from the neighborhood ought to be concerned for their safety, because bees weren't the sort to seek out children and sting them for no good reason. Because, she said—and although it was too dark to see her, and although I wasn't looking at her anyway, her voice made it clear that she was annoyed with me—because a bee really doesn't want to sting anyone. Because a sting is a life-ending choice for a bee. Because a bee's stinger is barbed on the stingy end and connected to internal organs on the other and to sting anything means that that bee will fly off mortally wounded. So, no, I'm not particularly worried about the children. She said the word children as though it were a little disgusting to her.

A bee stung me once, I said.

What?

When I was a kid. A bee stung my hand. It swelled up like a baseball glove. I think I'm allergic.

She didn't say anything for a long moment. Then she reached for her lamp, filling the room with subdued light that still felt harsh. You're allergic to bees? she asked.

Well, I said.

And you didn't tell me?

I don't know if I'm allergic, I said. It was a long time ago. I remember the doctor stressing that I had had an anaphylactic reaction rather than anaphylactic shock. There's a difference.

The doctor? she asked. You got stung by a bee and had to see a doctor?

I mean, I said, you should have seen my hand. Like a catcher's mitt, that thing.

Are you saying we can't have bees?

Sure, we can, I said. It's like you said. They don't want to sting anyone.

When I returned home from work the next day, a box was sitting on the kitchen counter.

It doesn't seem big enough to hold 10,000 bees, I said.

It really doesn't, my wife said.

We stared at the box for a long time, not saying anything.

After a while, my wife said she would return it first thing in the morning.

Why?

I just can't, she said. If you were to get stung.

Come on, I said. There are bees everywhere. Having a hive in our yard is hardly going to increase the risk. Plus, you bought all the stuff. I'll keep my distance while you put everything together. Hey, if it makes you feel better, I promise to never leave the house ever again.

She laughed at that.

It'll be fine, I said.

She nodded, wanting to be persuaded.

Are you sure?

We keep the bees, I said.

The next morning, my wife emptied the bees into their hive. Watching her do it from the safe distance of our kitchen, it really did look like she was pouring some dark liquid into that box. She looked funny in her oversized protective gear, but I could tell it made her happy just to be out there doing it.

Coming back toward the house, she removed her hood, and I opened the sliding glass door. She was beaming when she asked if I had been able to see the bees as she dropped them into the hive. I told her that I had and that it had been pretty amazing. It was then that I noticed a couple of bees on her suit, both near her shoulder. Here, I said, brushing them away.

Oh my, she said.

It's fine, I said.

This happened again later in the afternoon when a bee showed up in the kitchen and I waved it toward the open window. Several times over those next days, I used a drinking glass to catch bees that had wandered into the house. I slid a sheet of paper over the opening to trap a bee and then carried it outside, close to the hive, where I removed the paper and watched the bee fly away. Each time this happened, I marveled at the efficiency of bees. What fascinating little machines they were.

We put lawn chairs near the hive and just sat there with it most evenings. More than once, my wife said it made her nervous to have me so close to so many bees.

You know, I said, the more I think about it, I'm not sure it was a bee.

She looked at me and waited.

When I was a kid, I mean. It may have been a hornet.

Does it really matter? she said. I mean, if you're allergic to hornets aren't you also allergic to other striped stingy things?

I admitted that I didn't know if an allergy to one creature meant an allergy to another, and I said I would see what the internet had to say. For now, I said, isn't this nice? Isn't this lovely? We watched the way the bees flew in and out of their hive like planes at the world's busiest airport.

There was something about the hive that attracted me. I enjoyed the way it hummed, the way it made me feel I was part of something bigger. It wasn't long before I was coming home from work and heading straight outside.

At first, my wife checked the hive daily, taking the lid off to see how the colony was getting along. I noticed after a while that as she caught stray bees that had slipped into the house, she wasn't returning them to the hive anymore. Now, she was dumping them on the porch in a gesture that looked, to me, a little disdainful. The fact is that the hive took more work than my wife expected. She had thought—or we had—that the whole thing reduced to a simple matter of placing bees in a hive and setting them to their instinctive process. But my wife had a friend from work who began to quiz her about the care and attention she was giving her colony. This same friend had been the one to introduce her to beekeeping in the first place and had made it seem, my wife told me, like the easiest thing in the world. Now, my wife said, she's pestering me every day about checking for lost wax and what I'm doing to protect against pests and predators and wind and rain. It's just too much. She was tired, she said, of suiting up all the time.

I sympathized, recognizing the work of it all, and helped as I could. I began to read up on woodlice and mites. I found tips for fending off mice and raccoons and skunks. I learned all about supers, which gave the bees extra space to store honey, and excluders, which stopped the queen from laying eggs where we didn't want them. I started checking the hive daily for anything that needed repair. My wife would sit in the lawn chair and look on as I checked the hive. When I asked if the suit made me look fat, she said, You bet it does.

Sometimes, the conversation turned to pesticides and colony collapse and the virtues of planting fruit trees, but soon, she stopped coming outside quite so often.

One night, while we were eating dinner, I mentioned to my wife something I had read about honey. Did you know, I said, that honey has a terroir?

She made a noise to suggest she found this interesting.

Sure, I said. The soil, the climate, they have a real impact on the flavor of honey in a particular hive. And then, of course, the crops that the bees are visiting and cross-pollinating, that all makes a big difference, too. Bees near orange groves will make honey that carries some of that citrus flavor. Same goes for clover or buckwheat or whatever nectar the bees find.

Again, my wife made an interested sound, but I could see that she was focused on the table, something she saw there, which turned out to be a bee.

The bees had, through those several weeks, continued to find their way into the house. It happened most days at first and then every day. Sometimes it was just the one, sometimes several. We found them in the bathroom, in the living room, in our closet. And here we were, just finishing dinner and another bee was with us, there at the edge of the table. I reached for a glass, thinking to trap the thing when my wife smacked the bee with a flyswatter. She'd had it in her hand, and I hadn't even noticed. It surprised me more than a little and we both just sat there in silence for a bit before my wife finally stood and used a napkin to pick up the little bee carcass. As she did so, she said, quite casually, that she would be doing some grocery shopping the next day. Did I need anything?

The next morning, my wife mentioned her beekeeper friend from work. She wondered, the friend did, if my wife would be willing to sell her hive and colony.

Why would she ask that? I said.

Why wouldn't she?

I mean, why would she assume we wanted to get rid of our hive?

Our hive? she said.

The hive, I said.

She's coming later today to get everything, she said, and walked out of the room.

In the weeks after my wife's coworker loaded the hive and those 10,000 or more bees in a truck and hauled them away, we continued to find them everywhere. We assumed, at first, that these were the unlucky few who had been out on patrol when the hive was collected, but the numbers kept up and, strangely, seemed to increase. If they had been a small nuisance before, their presence in our house now became something worse. Where once we might have forgiven each bee, assuming it had lost its way, we now saw each one as an enemy soldier, the smallest part of an infestation. We would often find bees at our windows, knocking their heads pointlessly against the glass, but more and more often we found them dead and dying. Sometimes in our pantry, among the cereal boxes, sometimes in clusters in the hallway or at the base of the stairs. We took to vacuuming daily, using the various hose attachments we had never previously found a use for.

Sometimes, if I got home before my wife did, I would do a quick pass of the house, cleaning up the piles of bees I could find, and making sure the living ones got outside safely.

We were lying in bed one Saturday morning, talking about things we wanted to do with a wide-open day, when I noticed a small discoloration, maybe three or four inches across, on the ceiling right above my head. It was right where the ceiling met the wall. Worrying that it might be a leak in the roof, I went for my ladder to get a closer look. When I got close, though, and reached out to touch the spot, my fingers came away sticky and I immediately heard a humming, machine-like sound that had clearly been there all along. I must have screamed or yelled, because my wife, who had gone down to the kitchen, came running up the stairs. I stared at her and then at the spot and then back at her.

I think we have a problem, I said.

My wife called her friend from work who said that bees did sometimes build hives in houses but that it had never happened to her. She said this, my wife said, as though we, inexperienced keepers that we were, were clearly to blame. The coworker also said she had no expertise with this specific problem and suggested that we call the university, where they had a very fine entomology program and even a bee lab. They would know what to do, she assured my wife. A bee lab? my wife said to me, as though she wanted someone to get a load of this nonsense.

Instead of calling the university's bee lab, we contacted an exterminator who stood in our bedroom and stared at the ceiling for a while. The spot had grown darker in just the hours since we first noticed it and had taken on a soft shine. The exterminator said he could take care of it, no problem, but wouldn't we rather just set a jar on the bed and collect some fresh honey?

We stared at him for a moment and then he said, They're coming in from the eaves.

The eaves?

Come see, he said.

Outside, he pointed to the roof where, sure enough, the eaves and the rain gutter were covered in bees.

How did we miss that? I asked no one in particular.

They'll be sad to go, the exterminator said.

How long will it take? my wife asked

Well, the exterminator said, I think I could make it out here on Monday.

It's just that my husband, he's allergic.

The exterminator nodded at this while looking at me. Allergic, eh? I guess you should have thought of that before you turned on the vacancy sign. He chuckled a little.

Later, my wife and I talked about the exterminator, agreeing that he was a little nutty, but hopeful that he could do what we needed him to do.

What was that he said about a jar? I said.

Above us, a hive hummed.

The exterminator returned two days later, set up a ladder on the side of the house, and proceeded to use a series of power tools to saw away large portions of siding just below the eaves. We hadn't given permission for any sort of demolition, but what could we do? We didn't want bees living in our ceiling and this man seemed our best bet. This won't take long, he told us as he dropped a large piece of siding onto the ground. We get in here, grab that queen, and all these little guys will be perfectly happy to follow her anywhere. Easy peasy. He had with him a teenage boy who we learned was his youngest son.

When the exterminator finally removed the last of the siding, it looked like the house had an open wound. It was darker than I expected, and teeming with bees. The exterminator and his son suited up and took turns climbing the ladder, pulling away gooey bricks of honeycomb, searching each one for the queen, and then placing it in a large plastic bin. We watched all this from the safest distance we could find, swiping at the few bees zooming by.

When they were finished and packing up, it seemed to me that they'd left an awful mess behind, and a not-insignificant population of bees. I asked about all this, and I asked how they could be sure they got the queen.

Well, the exterminator said, we haven't seen her. Like *seen* seen her. But she's in one of these chunks, that's for sure. Don't you worry, we got her. You give this a day or two to settle down. The bees that are left will head off soon enough, looking for a new hive, then you'll want to get up there and mop up.

Mop up? I said.

Unless you're handy, you'll probably want to get a few bids on putting this all back together.

By the end of the week the exterminator was back, staring at the spot on our ceiling that had now grown to nearly a foot in diameter and was actively dripping. We had moved our bed and covered the ground with a tarp.

No jar? the exterminator said.

No jar, I said.

Where's your son? I asked.

Turns out he's allergic just like you, he said. Then, in a mock whisper, he said, That's what his mother says, but I don't buy it.

My wife started to say something, then stopped herself.

Well, the exterminator said, let's get to the bottom of this.

The three of us walked outside and stood shoulder to shoulder staring at the exposed hive which seemed, like the spot on our ceiling, to have grown.

Can you just get rid of the bees? my wife said.

Don't you worry, he said. Second time's a charm.

I bit my tongue.

It's a beautiful hive, the exterminator said. Probably started right after the house was built.

No, I said. It's new.

No, it's not.

I said, I mean we just bought a colony, and we think some of those bees decided to come into the house. So, just a couple months ago.

Nope, the exterminator said. Much older.

Can you just spray them? my wife said.

Could do, the exterminator said. You'd kill quite a few but make the rest angry. What you want is for these little fellas to want to leave. Just need to get the queen out.

I thought you took the queen already, I said.

Well, we hoped so, didn't we?

Really, my wife said, I'd just like to spray them.

Like I said, if we sprayed them, you'd ruin all the honey.

We don't want the honey, my wife said.

Boy, that's a lot of good honey, the exterminator said.

We left after that. We told the exterminator we wished him luck and said we'd be back later. We drove for an hour or more, got some lunch, and looked at a lake. When we got home, the exterminator was packing up.

Did you find the queen? I said.

Yep, he said. I sure hope so.

You hope so?

No way I missed her this time. Give it a day or two and you'll see.

We gave it a day or two and noticed, or thought we noticed, fewer bees swarming outside. We also thought the sound of the hive had diminished significantly, although we weren't sleeping in the bedroom by this point and didn't go up there any more than we had to. We were now sleeping in different rooms.

By the end of the week, we saw our wishful thinking for what it was. Outside, the hive moved in a way that reminded me of an oil slick. It purred with life.

We called the exterminator, and he was at our door in no time at all.

I'm just so sorry about this, he said.

He stood there with us, staring at the hive for a long time, sizing it up. She's in there somewhere, he said, though I don't think he meant for us to hear it.

Here's an idea, he said. I don't like to do it, but we could just kill the hive off. Hit it with some insecticide and problem solved.

My wife cleared her throat.

Wait, I said.

That sounds just fine, my wife said.

It'll take a few treatments, the exterminator said. I'll spray it today and come back tomorrow and the next day. By then, you'll be bee free. Hey, he said, Bee Free. That's a pretty good name for a company like mine. Don't steal it.

The other night, my wife and I sat on the patio and ate a light meal. It was only a salad, but we don't tend to be heavy eaters. My wife asked me how my day had been, and I asked about hers. Both, it turns out, had been fine. It's early October now and fall has announced itself. The leaves in the hills have turned and like every year at this time, the evening gets just a bit cooler than we expect. We talked about the weather, how lovely it was, and the leaves, too, but for long stretches we ate in silence. We've been married a long while now and we don't always feel a need to say things. We certainly didn't feel a need to talk about the exterminator or the mess he made or what he finally charged us.

As we were finishing our salad, a bee landed on the edge of the table. It didn't seem particularly interested in our food. It just sat there, its body vibrating like an idling car. I imagined its tiny bee heart pumping away. I looked at my wife who was staring intently at a tomato she had skewered with her fork.

Quietly, trying not to be noticed, I slid my hand closer to the bee. When it didn't move to fly away, I placed my cupped hand over it.

My wife asked if there was anything better than an October evening.

I said there wasn't.

She asked if I would mind clearing the table.

Of course, I said.

I pretended to wipe away crumbs, shooing the bee toward the yard. As I did so, I felt a pinch in the palm of my hand.

Was something the matter, my wife wanted to know.

No, I said. It's nothing.

As I gathered up plates and forks, I noticed that my hand felt warm and tight and that my palm was beginning to itch.

Rosenvall's Cage

There's Haggarty saying that he knows of a girl who looks, at twenty-three, like something from a zombie movie. Saying the girl could look no worse, that her body will manage no more scarring. Saying she is exactly what she is, and that her photograph in a pamphlet reminds teenagers to think twice before drinking and driving.

There's grass: dead in some spots, dying in others. A motor home for sale. Vinyl siding. Mowing strips. Tomato cages, tomato plants, tomatoes. A ground-level deck that hasn't seen a coat of stain in five summers. A wheelbarrow. A roll of chain-link fencing leaning against a pile of bricks. Weeds, broken trellises, and a rusting barbecue grill. These two men: Rosenvall inside a cage, Haggarty not. Rosenvall asking Haggarty to be a champ and hand over that wrench in the toolbox. Haggarty saying again that it's so damn hot. These two men who have known each other only long enough to establish that one is, in fact, *the* Rosenvall who escapes from things, and that the other used to write speeding tickets.

Haggarty with his gut. Haggarty who used to be a state trooper. Haggarty who can't stop saying how hot it is. Not just hot, but really hot. Wanting to know if it always gets this hot, because he can't remember heat like this, and because there's hot and then there's hot, but this is something else. Not wanting to overstate the point, but this has got to be some record. Damn, he says, wondering aloud if a thermometer can be trusted in this heat. Wondering if Rosenvall's daughter is bringing more lemonade.

Rosenvall, sweating. Rosenvall wishing he had an impact driver. Rosenvall whose wrist is acting up, noticing there's more to do than has been done. Rosenvall who's happy enough to take the lemonade his daughter offers. Rosenvall who's building himself a cage just too large for the neighbors to the south, the ones who complain about property value and say that there are certain restrictions, that a man can't simply build a building wherever he chooses. Had he thought of that? Had he thought of permits?

Haggerty asking how Rosenvall ended up here. Rosenvall saying that it's a long story, a story for another day. Saying he realized one day how little he knew, how insignificant he was. In a world that kept changing, what need was there for his kind of escape? He lost the art, or it lost him. That, too, was a long time ago. Ten or twenty years, at least. What Rosenvall tells Haggarty is that once the curtain fell, he was only a U-Haul away from anywhere, and this place is no better or worse than any other.

Haggarty saying this place isn't so bad. Nice place to raise a family. Saying his wife and kids mean everything. Asking Rosenvall if he has kids other than the daughter who lives here, in this house, whose lemonade is so welcome on a day like today. Haggarty looking over his own fence from the wrong side, watching his house, his back to Rosenvall. This heat, he says, this heat.

Haggarty talking about this kid without arms and legs. A kid who doesn't know yet that his chances of living are smaller than small. I mean, seriously, Haggarty says, this kid doesn't even know that his arms are like 200 feet away, burning in the wreckage, and his legs are all mangled. But he's smiling, this kid. Like he's proud of himself. Why was he smiling? It's ugly stuff, Haggarty says. It's not the stuff you see in any office, or in some law firm. No way, Haggarty says. There's no way you can tell me that anybody anywhere has seen the things I've seen. There's sweat rolling from his forehead like he's the one building a cage. Like he's doing anything but chatting up the day.

Rosenvall's nose, bent at the bridge. His left ear, lower than his right. The way he limps a little, like a man who wouldn't know how not to limp. His voice restricted in range and unlikely to soothe a stranger. The scars on his arms from burns and lacerations. The way he denies the metaphor of escape, saying that his cage is only a cage. It doesn't mean anything.

Haggarty saying that maybe Rosenvall could teach him a thing or two. That maybe when this cage is done they can get started on one for him. Haggarty asking if there are lessons. Are there steps? Is there some rule about wearing black all the time even when it's so damn hot, and there's no shade, and the lemonade is great but is there more? Because he's always up for something new. He could be the guy who escapes the heat. Huh? Haggarty says. Huh? What does Rosenvall think of his neighbor's quick wit? Haggarty saying he's no weatherman, but this is some heat.

Rosenvall and a glass of water at three in the morning in his daughter's living room.

The colorful books that fill uneven shelves. Many have Rosenvall's name on them. Rather, they have Rosenvall's daughter's name on them. These books have been a living for her. The means by which she bought this house and got herself into that photograph of the Eiffel Tower, standing before it with a woman, a friend of hers. She says her books aren't for reading, they're for buying. The sort parents collect for their children even if the children didn't ask. Books children will open, if ever, for a school report on space exploration, volcanoes, the industrial revolution. Like encyclopedias, she says, but not so heavy. Rosenvall pulls from the shelf a volume dedicated to sea creatures that will kill you without even trying. The blue-ringed octopus (*Hapalochlaena fasciata*) makes its rounds in the shallows, in the reefs and tide pools off Japan and Australia, secreting a venom that kills slowly but only after causing nausea, paralysis, and blindness.

Rosenvall's daughter saying, Dad, I know I told you you could build this thing in my yard, I know I said you could do what you wanted out there, but listen. Her neighbors have been calling, and they have questions. Really dad, could you at least let them talk? Pretend to listen? I don't know what to tell them anymore when they ask what you're building. She says that her neighbors want to believe that this thing will be a garage or a shed. Easier to ignore once the exterior is complete. They worry about property values, and who can blame them?

A clock on the wall. At the top of each hour, a different song by a different North American bird. At this hour, the house finch (*Haemorhous mexicanus*). Rosenvall sipping at a glass of water, nursing it like he can't afford another. His daughter sitting next to him, with a posture to suggest she'll only sit for a minute before standing, running her hands through her hair, saying something about how late it is, returning down the darkened hallway to her room. Rosenvall refusing to meet his daughter's eyes as she watches him. He nods, confirming that he has heard but admitting nothing, acknowledging only that he was here for this conversation. His daughter's two hands rested on one of his. I don't need you to stop, Dad. I just need you to be nice.

What Rosenvall will tell his daughter later, when both of them have had more sleep, when she's returned from work, the worst of the heat come and gone, is that he understands how important it is that she not offend anyone, and how much he admires her for being kind, but making people uneasy is what he does best. She says, Sure Dad, but these people didn't ask for a show.

Rosenvall and his daughter sitting together over pork loin, cooked carrots, green salad. The song of the Cape May Warbler (*Setophaga tigrina*) because it's six o'clock. Nearby, a miniature statue of the tower at Pisa, a spoon from Bruges mounted to a placard, a small Union Jack in a vase of silk daisies. Nearly everything in sight comes from travels in Western Europe. A gift shop. The evidence of tourism. He doesn't know how it happened without his noticing, but at some point his daughter became a real traveler. She says a lot of things happen when you aren't there to see them. He wants to know what exactly she means by that. She says she meant nothing, that she's tired. She's glad he's here with her now.

Rosenvall's daughter's body has aged while she wasn't looking. She spends too much time arranging food on her plate before she eats a forkful of everything at once. She squints to adjust her glasses instead of tilting her head half an inch to adjust her line of sight. She's taken no great care of her hands, allowing calluses and dry weather to have their way.

Dad, listen. When the neighbors talk about this thing in my yard, they call it by all sorts of names, and I know that I should correct them, but I don't know how. So, tell me, what is it? Is it temporary? A means to an end? Do you mean to lock yourself inside? Rosenvall doesn't have an answer. He looks past his daughter, sidelong, licking his dry lips. Yeah, he says, I don't know that I know. He thought he knew in the beginning, but things have changed, gotten confused. He says it was a simple enough plan, that he meant to get himself in shape, a little practice, refine his skills, but now, what he has now is a cage worth less than the materials he used to make.

Rosenvall's daughter saying she remembers going to see his show once, years ago, when it was her birthday, and she convinced her mother that she should see him again. Rosenvall staring back, asking when this was. His daughter rifling through an old shoebox, pulling out stacks of photos but not the one she's looking for, the one, she says, where she's standing next to the overlarge picture of Rosenvall. She says, I wanted to go backstage, to see you. But that had been too much for her mother, for the woman who said sorry, the deal was to come this far and no farther. They saw the show, thought it was fun, and went home with a postcard.

There's Haggarty talking about a family of four in a minivan, wearing seatbelts, driving safely. How a seventeen-year-old kid, high on marijuana, driving into the sun, lost control of his truck, came across the median, collided head on. Haggarty pausing for effect, waiting to reveal who died and who didn't. Father, mother, daughter: dead. But not infant son, and not the kid high on marijuana. See, Haggarty says, it's like I'm always saying, these kids don't know anything. No way in the world this kid should be alive, but there it is. Went through a windshield, you bet he did, and he'll limp the rest of his life, but alive. The family on the other hand, the poor family. Haggarty asking Rosenvall what he knows about the jaws of life, what he knows about helicopters that go where no ambulance can. Rosenvall admitting that he knows very little.

Haggarty's shirt revealing the way his body sweats. The way moisture spreads from under the arms, down the back, around the waist. Out of his air-conditioned home not ten minutes and already drenched. Sweat forms on his forehead and drops appear one at a time on the tip of his nose, growing until the weight becomes too much. He asks Rosenvall how long he's been performing, if the routine weighs on him, if he considers retirement. Because seriously, Haggarty says, these last months, now that I'm home and not working, have been the best of my life. Haggarty admitting that he and Rosenvall have had very different careers, but still, he knows what he knows, and retirement has been a joy so far.

Rosenvall staring back. Rosenvall saying that the audience always thinks he's safer than he is, that they can't see the medics just off stage. Saying that no one would guess just how dangerous his act is. They applaud wildly for him and yet can't know just how close he comes to death each night. Rosenvall saying that the applause goes to his head sometimes. Like, for example, when he stands on a platform above a glass tank filled with water and sharks. There's music, an assistant, the voice of an emcee announcing that what Rosenvall is about to do is very dangerous, very difficult, and as likely to kill him as anything he has ever done. There's that long moment, standing there on the platform, water swirling below him, watching the hungry sharks made active by a bucket of chum. Rosenvall saying that nothing compares to that moment, nothing compares to the applause from an audience he can never see through the stage lights.

Rosenvall's daughter coming out through the back door. Rosenvall saying that he's done. Almost done. Rosenvall saying that he didn't expect it to take this long, but that it turned out better than he had hoped. Rosenvall turning to his daughter. She says she doesn't know what to say, she really has no idea what to say. Rosenvall starting to explain that she doesn't have to say anything, but his daughter continuing that she would like to know what it is before she says something she'll regret because she thought her father was building a cage back here, but this is no cage, because a cage has an inside, and this thing doesn't. Rosenvall saying that maybe if she moves a few feet to her left. His daughter moving, saying, yes, she can see better, but still this is nothing like anything she's ever seen. Haggarty moving as well. Haggarty agreeing that this is a cage. Saying he wasn't going to say anything, but he's been wondering for a while now.

Rosenvall's cage is, in fact, seven cages. Like nesting dolls, it's one cage larger than the next, one cage overwhelming the last. It's a cage too small for one man, encompassed by another cage and another and then four more. The bars are close enough together, and offset from one cage to the next, so that, from certain angles it's nearly impossible to see anything more than a black metal cube. From another angle, standing just where Rosenvall's daughter and Haggarty stand now, the cage nearly disappears, reduced to one set of bars, about three inches apart, like the door of a prison cell.

Rosenvall saying that the external frame was simple enough, but it required another and then another. He doesn't remember how it happened, but before he knew it, he had a cage of cages, and it didn't take long to see that it wasn't many things, but one thing in many parts. Rosenvall's daughter saying she thinks it's great that he's done and that he's happy with it. Rosenvall asking her to try just a bit harder to sound interested. Saying that this is the greatest thing he's ever built. Saying that he finally made the cage he always wanted, the cage that he couldn't begin to understand. His daughter saying she knows he can get out of the cage, but what she really wants to know is how he means to get in it. Rosenvall saying it's impossible, that it can't be done. His daughter saying she knows it can't be done, but wonders how he's going to do it anyway. Rosenvall saying no, that she's missing the point. His daughter asking that he give her a buzz when he figures things out, throwing up her hands, disappearing into the house.

Haggarty saying he saw this program on television. There were sharks and these underwater cages where men with cameras could observe them. Those cages were smaller than this by a mile. But still, Haggarty says, strong enough to keep a shark out. Haggarty saying he gets a little claustrophobic in a tight space, and that's why the open road was always where he wanted to be. But even there, he saw things that shook him. For example, Haggarty saw more fatalities than he cares to remember. He saw how disregard for safety was nearly always where it started. He saw things that still make his skin crawl. Come to think of it, Haggarty can remember more than a few cases where the reckless driver was the one who survived. Like that kid, he says. No seatbelt and he's the one to live. Always the idiots who limp away.

Later. Rosenvall's daughter standing at the door, saying she's sorry but that she just sees that thing in her yard as a thing she's going to have to get rid of, saying she knows it means a lot to him, but that it's not something he can fit in a suitcase, and what does he expect her to do with it when he leaves. Rosenvall shaking his head slowly, starting to say something, his daughter cutting him off, saying, Come on, Dad. Waiting for a response that doesn't come, saying, You can't stay here. Rosenvall asking what she means, asking if she means that he isn't welcome or isn't capable. Rosenvall's daughter saying it hardly matters.

Later. Midnight. Haggarty saying that he's definitely not the one who would know, but for his money it seems like a fine cage. Maybe not so good for sharks, but it seems sturdy. Rosenvall staring past his cage, staring like he has, on and off, for hours. Haggarty trying again to get a response, trying again to be good company, saying how odd it is that the two of them are sitting here, in the middle of the night. Saying that he doesn't sleep so well because his wife insists on cutting the air conditioning at sundown, and that his house is an oven. Saying he wouldn't have guessed the sun had been down for hours already, and that he's beginning to understand what it must be like for those people in Greenland or Alaska or wherever it is that the sun doesn't go down for months at a time. Saying that he could stand a little cool air to go along with his sun. Saying this heat is killing him. Wondering if he's alone here. Asking if Rosenvall feels how hot it is, at midnight. Rosenvall nodding, smiling a little, saying that he feels it, too, but what can you do?

Haggarty telling Rosenvall about the woman he found burning in her own car, wedged between the steering wheel and her door, her seatbelt having saved her only for a worse death, how she'd swerved to dodge a drowsy driver, how she must have been conscious through every roll her car took. Haggarty saying he doesn't miss it most days. Saying he sometimes feels haunted by it. Saying he feels guilty but can't say why.

Rosenvall saying nothing. Haggarty saying nothing.

There's Rosenvall's cage in the warm half-light of early morning. There's the way its size is difficult to judge for the shadows. It might be massive, big as a house, or nothing more than a shadow itself. There's the sound of automatic sprinklers kicking on, the quick expulsion of air from underground pipes, rushing water broken into thousands of parts. Water runs down the bars of Rosenvall's cage, pooling at its base where it waits to be absorbed into the impossible soil. The cycle repeats four times daily and still the grass yellows, still it dies and dies and never stops dying, still the water batters the frame of Rosenvall's cage, as if one of them must win, as if this cage were something other than what it is.

Age, Epoch, Era, Eon

At fifteen, as his coach hits fungos far into the blue, blue sky, the center fielder doesn't know and cannot be expected to know that his father's days are numbered. He doesn't know that all too soon, on a day much like this one, his mother will arrive on time to pick him up from practice. That he will get into the car as he always does. That he will say nothing. That he will wait for her to drive forward, to head for home. That she will sit too long, idle too long, begin to cry. That she will try but fail to give him the news quickly.

Except for in the broadest possible terms, the center fielder doesn't know what his father does each day, each morning. He doesn't know what it means to commute more than ninety minutes deep into the open emptiness of eastern Utah. He doesn't know what it means to enter the mouth of the mine, to descend so many hundreds of feet, to be reminded, too often, that a mountain rises above you, its full weight supported by ever-narrower columns of coal.

The center fielder doesn't yet know that he has asthma or that it's induced by allergies and exertion. He hasn't yet felt the full weight of that disease, the full panic he'll be under when he does. He doesn't know that the cut grass all around his feet is the primary reason his eyes have begun to water, his throat to itch, the palms of his hands to tingle so slightly. He doesn't yet know that this is the last year he'll play organized ball. That his season will end on a poorly hit grounder to third. That he won't touch a bat again for a decade. That he won't encourage his sons to play, won't ever ask them to have a throw.

The center fielder doesn't know that on May 1, 1900, the fourth shaft of the Winter Quarters mine exploded, killing 200 men. Or that the citizens in the nearby town of Scofield heard the noise and, in at least some cases, mistook it for fireworks celebrating Dewey Day. Or that there were no more than 125 caskets available in Salt Lake City. That the rest were shipped from Denver. Or that there were two funeral services on May 5: one held at the Lutheran church, the other at the Mormon. Or that the explosion left some men alive, but that the afterdamp still had them dying, suffocating. That it was, at the time, the worst mining disaster in the history of the United States. That it is, now, fifth on that list. Or that the 200 dead was an estimate some considered low. Or that President William McKinley wired to say he felt deep sympathy for the wives and children of the victims, and that he felt intense sorrow when he heard news of the terrible calamity. That the dead men left no fewer than 107 widows, 270 children. Or that one man lost two brothers in the accident and, having been in Abercarn in 1878, insisted that that other disaster was tame compared to this one.

The center fielder didn't know, until his coach explained, that an aluminum fungo bat could hit a lobbed ball farther than any standard bat, but that it would bend in half around a fast pitch. He doesn't know that his coach, this too-fat man who insists on wearing his too-tight uniform even to practices, is as happy as he could ever hope to be. Happy to be the father of four healthy daughters. Happy to have a job that pays him to be outside. Happy to know a handful of young men who have excelled at this sport and thank him for his role in their achievement.

He knows nothing of Standardville, of Kennilworth, of Sunnyside. He knows nothing of Castle Gate, every bit as fierce as Scofield. He knows of Wilberg, but too little. He can't yet know of Crandall Canyon. The center fielder can't see the future. He can't know what awaits him. He can't guess at what lies there, lurking. He can't yet see the mine as a place for him. He can't know that what is not an option now will become the only option soon enough. What choice will he have? Just out of high school, a father too soon, where else is he to go?

The center fielder doesn't know how he knows to track and catch a fly ball. He doesn't know when he developed an eye for the height and angle and velocity of an object coming off a bat 300 feet away. Or the sound it makes when hit cleanly, solidly. He doesn't know when he developed the instinct for a good jump, this knack for knowing without knowing how or why, without thought, without explanation. Or when he learned to pace his run, timing it just so, arriving with the ball, catching it in stride. He doesn't know when he learned to judge the size of the batter, the speed of the swing, the force of the breeze, the density of the air, the length of the grass. He doesn't know when he came to trust the high arc of a ball hit deep to center, its unnamed mathematics, its unfailing reliability. The most perfect thing in the universe.

He doesn't know that he only has to look to his grandfather's generation to find the pick-and-shovel miners that seem to him the stuff of legend. Or that they thought of themselves as farmers first, miners second. That they grew alfalfa, yes, and wheat, and maybe corn for silage. That they raised no more than forty or fifty head of beef cattle. That to lose a calf was something terrible, hundreds of dollars gone, a season lost. Or that his father milked a cow every night, helped his grandmother clean eggs before she sold them, thirty-six dozen at a time, to the Draper Egg Company. That he lived without television until he was fourteen. That they were poor but didn't know it. Or that his father went to the mines long before he was old enough to work inside them, packing bags of sand for the explosives team.

The center fielder knows or ought to know that coal is his state's official rock. That it's a fossil fuel. That at one point in the planet's history, large swamps covered much of the earth's surface. That trees, bushes, ferns, and other plant life photosynthesized the rays of the sun, and stored all that light, all that energy. That these plants and the ground they grew in were periodically covered in landslides, earthquakes, floods, creating dense pockets of rich organic matter. That it formed a nutrient-rich peat moss that was preserved and compressed and heated for millions of years. That ribbons of coal might be found throughout America, just beneath America, in the substrata of America. That this place he calls home is not even among the top ten producers in the nation. He doesn't know that a continuous mining machine can excavate as much coal in one day as a team of men given a month. He can't possibly know that his father will soon become caught, stuck, trapped, wedged between a continuous miner and a wall of bituminous coal half a billion years old. That he will be fully six hundred feet beneath the barren surface when it happens. That those who see it will say there was nothing that could have stopped it, that no one was at fault, that it was a terrible, terrible accident.

They will tell him, in the weeks and months that follow, that his father seemed to know what was going to happen, to sense it. That he said his goodbyes even if he was unaware of doing so. That he systematically contacted nearly everyone he knew and cared about, everyone who was or ought to have been dear to him, and spent a few minutes, a few hours, an afternoon, maybe, with those he should have seen more often but rarely did. That he returned to the fields with his father and his uncle, if only for that one weekend. That they said very little as they stacked hay. That that weekend seems to them now some touch of the divine.

He knows little of mining. He knows nothing of the room and pillar system that makes a world of that underworld, a system so old and so familiar that it might as well be another century in those depths. He knows nothing of the arguments for smaller and smaller pillars. Of the risks. Of the retreat they make when a mine is allowed, systematically, to collapse upon itself, to crash down with all the terrible force of the great world above it.

He doesn't recognize that his hands are too soft and too weak, unaccustomed to real labor. That he has never, in any real sense, worked the land. The center fielder's eyes itch and he rubs them, feels them begin to water and swell. He knows to anticipate this, knows he will regret touching them. Knows, too, that the roof of his mouth, his palate, will ache in the morning if he forces his tongue up against it, if he satisfies the itch there as he wants to, as he's helpless not to. His ears have filled with that deadened sound of so much congestion. His nostrils sting from dry cracking.

The center fielder has already forgotten the day, weeks gone, when Mr. Blackwell in earth science held up a fist-sized piece of coal and asked if anyone knew what it was. He's already forgotten that he had thought to answer but decided not to. He's forgotten that Mr. Blackwell said that coal was primarily carbon, but that it also contained nitrogen, hydrogen, sulfur, and oxygen. Coal, he said, was responsible for the very electricity running through the walls of the school. Coal, he said, as though the word were its own proof, as though it were all that needed saying. He turned the lights off and then on, off and then on, an illustration of his point.

He hasn't yet heard that thing his father has tried to tell him so many times. He hasn't paid attention when his father jokes that his first conscious thought was a desire to get the hell out of this place. He hasn't listened to his father's indirect advice to choose a life other than this one. To take the opportunity while the opportunity exists. He hasn't listened when his father complains about the dangers of a life like this one, the risks one takes. A place where one must fight, scratch and claw, beg for a job that might kill you.

He knows only that it's late in the evening before his father comes in the back door. He knows only that his father will be gone again long before the rest of the family wakes in the morning. He doesn't know that the silence filling the house is something he will soon regret. He doesn't know that tomorrow or the next day or the next will be the last time his father sits at this table, the last time he might ask an empty question about what happened at school that day. He knows only that coal is a thing one mines, a thing one burns, a thing one relies on. It has not yet occurred to him that coal is a thing held jealously by the earth. He will know soon enough. He will know as well as any man has ever known. But not today. Not yet.

The Trees in North America

1

And so, in the spring of her twenty-first year, the bandages come off and nearly everything returns to the way it had been. Delores hears stories, and many of them, about soldiers with purple hearts and survivors of horrific accidents disappointed to continue their lives without certain appendages. These stories, without exception, end on a note of affirmation. Has she heard about the man who lost his leg and became a marathon runner? The double Dutch champion with only one foot? The water skier with no arms? All true, she's told to remember. Lemonade from lemons.

Unlike certain veterans, Delores doesn't wake after long nights with a phantom pain where one of her fingers used to be, her body remembering its former self, generating sensation where a finger once was. The fingers on her left hand are gone, gone completely, and it seems that her body has neatly forgotten them. But she still has her right hand with its full complement, and she has her left thumb, which should be good for something.

What she tells her mother is that she feels angry for the loss, and that she blames herself for allowing this to happen. What she tells her boyfriend, Dale, is that she regrets the things she won't be able to do now. She'll never again ride a bicycle comfortably, never hold a phone in one hand and write with the other, never applaud as vigorously. Dale says that he understands but that it isn't so bad, not if she sets her mind to living the way she wants to live and not allowing herself to feel, always, resigned to something else. She never cared about riding a bicycle before, Dale says. But look, Delores says back, I'll never wear a wedding ring. Although he could suggest that her right hand is good enough, or that rings are part of a pointless, backward, archaic tradition, he gives up and goes quiet right when she wishes he wouldn't.

I'll never hold a baby, Delores tells her mother, not the way a baby needs to be held. And she won't be able to wear gloves either, not the way they need to be worn, or snap the fingers of both her hands at the same time. She also won't be able to read a book with the same ease she's come to expect or wear as many pitted olives on her fingertips come Thanksgiving.

She can enjoy the time she won't spend in the garden. At least she has that excuse now. She can hardly be expected to manipulate those tools. Her father tries to convince her that she needs to do what she's always done, no matter how awkward, that she needs to be stronger than her loss. But he seems unable to separate himself from his long familiar language of green thumbs and clichés about what's on one hand and what's on the other. It doesn't matter, though. Delores is resolved to regret the things she doesn't have. Having wanted them before is beside the point.

She plays the carpenter's saw like a cello, and she plays it more frequently and with greater attention now, having decided that this, of all things, is something she can embrace despite her missing fingers. She's happy to remind anyone who asks just how difficult an instrument it is to play. It should be apparent, she says, that while the difficulty has increased, the quality of her playing has not diminished. She wonders if they've heard about the woman who lost her fingers but still made a thirty-inch handsaw sing. She's determined, even as she mothers her regrets, to prove that an incomplete hand can still produce beautiful music, and she's not about to advertise that the musical saw requires less of her left hand than a piano or a guitar does. Instead, she's prepared an elaborate response for anyone who might challenge her achievement, suggesting that she hasn't overcome all that much, that unlike certain athletes she hasn't chosen a medium that allows her to succeed against probability. She knows she won't get the chance to say what she has in mind because no one is likely to make such a challenge. If there's some consolation in not feeling an unbearable itch in a finger she no longer has, she sometimes wonders if she wouldn't prefer it. Wouldn't it allow her, however briefly, to imagine that everything was the way it used to be?

Dale says, You should have seen her, you really should have seen her. He says Delores was the best guitar player he had ever seen, and he's seen his share. He's seen the best of the best and he knows what he's talking about, and he means it when he says that Delores was good. Delores says, You're embarrassing me.

Dale says he isn't disappointed in the saw. The saw is a wonderful and beautiful instrument and he's no expert or anything, but he thinks she's probably the best saw player in the world. She smiles when he says this because she knows he means it and that he's wrong but that he's doing the best he can. She knows that as a guitar player she was important to Dale and that now she's only someone he loves. No small thing that, but it's still less than what it was before. She'd been a girlfriend, yes, but a collaborator too, and she was involved in everything that mattered to him. She might strum a chord now, but who can't? If it had been her other hand, if she had lost the fingers on her right hand, she might be able to fake it. But this is wrong, too, just as useless. Instead, she's found herself more inclined to hide away. She goes to Dale's shows less often. Because it's easy to be a fan, she says. When Dale reminds her that she's so much more than some groupie, it only makes things worse.

Her father, Archie, is a large man who manages, because of his profession, to talk about Delores's body like it doesn't belong to her. He says, The fingers are not as vital as you might think, not like the liver or the uterus. He means well, she knows, but sensitivity is something different for him. He says, I mean, think about it. This while he's standing on a ladder, as Delores hands him a small tree saw, and after she has said, They're my fingers, and before she asked if he's sure that planting a tree in the living room is really such a good idea. He says, Tell me this won't look great. He claims to have taken structural integrity—both the tree's and the house's—into account. It's not as if he plans on moving any time soon and why would he do something that would damage his house, where he eats and sleeps, where he raised his family? No, he says, This is going to look great. Trust me. She does trust him, she tells him so, and she wonders what her mother will think each autumn when it comes to raking the living room. And the aphids, had he thought of them or whatever insects this tree is sure to bring with it? It's not as if the cherry trees didn't invite enough bugs already. At least it's not a box elder, he says. Think of that.

Archie got the idea in a pancake house in California. Although that tree was an enormous and thriving elm around which the pancake house had been built, he says that this tree, a green ash, should do quite well inside the house, where it will get more oxygen, and where it will be as easy to care for and ignore as a piece of furniture. Cold winters will do less damage to an indoor tree, he says, but that's only one of the benefits.

Delores watches as her father weatherproofs the enormous hole he has put in his ceiling and crawl space and roof. She says, What about us? Isn't this like leaving a door open all year? Archie says he's taken the weather into account, too, and that before the autumn comes, he will devise a means of keeping the house warm despite the hole. For now, he says, a tarp will keep any rain out and, isn't it time for lunch?

Delores's mother, Ruby, spends most of her time in the garden. It's not yet mid-June and already she's digging up something where she means to plant something else. No one likes a dying flower, Ruby says. She comes into the house with dirt under her fingernails and a bunch of late tulips that she places in a vase on the kitchen table where Delores and Archie are just sitting down over egg-salad sandwiches.

The problem with nature, Archie is saying, is that we like to think we can live outside it. This is nothing new to Delores or Ruby who have heard, countless times, his various lectures. He's currently about to argue that if people will only embrace nature more fully and really live in it, they will see, we will all see, that lives have improved. That this is a simultaneous defense for his current project and a plea for bringing more trees indoors is both transparent and—Ruby is likely to say—not going to get him anywhere soon, because one tree is enough, and until she's convinced that that one tree can be kept insect-free, she's not at all confident it will stay. The problem with nature, Ruby says instead, is weeds. Delores's younger brother, Christopher, has just stepped into the room and it seems to Delores that it's a little late in the day to be rubbing sleep from one's eyes. Christopher is, nonetheless, newly awake and not too happy about it. He's seventeen and annoyed by pretty much everything.

Speaking of weeds, Ruby says, why did I find so many around the tomato cages this morning? Christopher shrugs and says he must have pulled a thousand weeds yesterday and that he's sorry but that there's no way he could get to them all. He rolls his eyes at no one.

Among the things Christopher is not apathetic to are punk rock and the rate at which certain reptiles regrow severed limbs. It's not surprising to Delores that her brother would have such an interest in reptiles considering that their father is a high school biology teacher. Having a father in such a profession has its advantages. Christopher has had access to pets that none of his friends could rival. Although the interest in constricting snakes and horned toads and very small alligators has worn off most boys by the time they hit late adolescence, Christopher has continued to collect all sorts of scaled and/or burrowing pets.

Delores, who has never shared her brother's interest in creeping things, has not found her father's job so rewarding. After all, he was the first adult most of her friends ever heard use words like erection, intercourse, and vagina. Although the frankness that so embarrassed Delores in high school is also what endears her to her father today. She's never seen him blush.

2

Archie has chosen the green ash because it's a hardwood, and because he knows it will grow better than most hardwoods in this climate, and because he doesn't have time to wait for an oak. He's not doing this for posterity but for himself, and so he wants a tree that can get off to a quick start. He knows, still, that even a fast-growing tree is nothing to sit around and watch, but he's as patient as he's likely to get, and his perfect health is hardly something he can count on forever.

He's a solid and heavy sleeper whose snoring is like a jackhammer. His family has grown accustomed to the enormous noise he makes at night, and they have long since stopped making jokes about it. Despite how deeply he sleeps, he doesn't often stay asleep through the night. He wakes too often to pee or to get a drink or just to wait until he's tired again. Sometimes, in the middle of the night, if he can't get back to sleep, Archie will hear Delores playing music in her room. Through the kitchen, it's the same notes over and over. Weeks ago, he could have named the songs, could have whistled along. He's no expert, to be sure, but he knows a thing or two, and the songs she used to play were as familiar as the jingles on television. These days, he's finding it harder to identify the sounds through the wall. Delores doesn't seem to be returning to the country music she embraced for so long, and since her guitar playing has come to an end, she's also stopped listening to her once-favorite records. The classical music is nice, Archie says. Nicer than the country, but these new variations are hard to like. He tells Delores this and then reminds her that he doesn't know much about music, but some things just sound nice and some things don't, and he's just talking, whatever it's worth.

She's told him, repeatedly, that things are different for her now, that she sees her missing fingers as a constant reminder that she can't go backward. Archie is confused by his daughter's behavior. The music she plays now, on a saw that his grandfather left him, is unadorned and dark. She plays cycles of notes, like scales, with only small variations for what might be hours. She tells him it's her attempt to strip music to its elements, to find something beautiful in a spare repetition. Like certain words, she tells him. Like certain words repeated too often. Or the way your very home can feel foreign when you wake up from a strange dream. This, Archie admits, is something he understands.

Archie has always liked Dale. So, he's disappointed, though he won't say so, when he hears him explain that the musical saw is not exactly what he had in mind. Dale says he knows that many great country bands have featured saws, and that many of his favorite albums spotlight some terrific saw playing, but he has trouble imagining his band finding a place for the instrument. His is not the downbeat country of certain cover bands but something more spirited and lively. Dale says this to Delores late at night, when she gives him back his guitar and says, It won't do me much good. Archie excuses himself from the room when he can see that something significant is about to happen: a breakup or reconciliation. He's unsurprised, some moments later, to hear Delores's voice raised slightly.

Archie has taught high school juniors for nearly twenty-five years. What started as a summer job gradually became a profession. And now, with a little hindsight, he sees that he's not cut out for this sort of thing. Not that there's anything he or anyone can do about it now. He finds himself tired of the repetition, tired of the students coming to him each year with the same disinterest. That he was recently voted teacher of the year might have meant something a decade ago, but he's been bored for a long time.

Initially, he approached the beginning of each school year with a sense of excitement, like he had a chance to change the world, turning students on to some ideas that they'd never even considered. He had to teach them about their bodies, sure, but he didn't have to make it tedious. His students, he'd thought, were learning about the wonders of the human machine and the natural world. If only one of them went on to a career in marine biology, or medicine, or anthropology, he thought, he would count himself successful. That none of them ever did was only one of his disappointments. What also got to him was the ease with which he could identify his students on the first day of the year. The smart ones, the needy ones, the clowns, the ones who would blush at the mention of a reproductive organ. He could know, with some certainty, who was going to struggle before he knew their names. It didn't help that their names were always the same. How many Emily's did the world need?

He stands in front of a new batch of students and says, We're going to use words like penis in this class. Since his is not an elective course, Archie can tell his students—with some authority—to please get used to the idea. He stands in front of his students and gives them their first assignment: to collect and identify by name (common and Latin) the seeds of twenty-five different trees. He gives them an enormously long time to complete this assignment (six weeks) and says, Please try to find at least one tree that doesn't grow anywhere near your house. He knows, of course, that they'll have to go beyond their own backyards, but they're not likely to get any farther than the local nursery.

Ruby says, The problem with nature is weeds. By which she means to say that her job as a florist would be made easier if not for the weeds that grow, inevitably, wherever flowers will grow and even where they will not. Archie has heard this before. He says, The problem is not the weeds but our perception of them, by which he means to suggest that there really is no such things as a weed, but that among things that grow, there are some that please us and some that do not, and those things that do not please us we call weeds. Ruby says, If I can't sell it, it's a weed. If it grows, uninvited, in my flower beds, it's a weed. By which she means exactly what she said. This conversation is nearly automatic now and gets shorter each time they have it.

Archie feels responsible for nature. He feels that it's his job, despite whatever ineffectiveness, to remind people that we're not alone on this planet, and that horrendous injustices to the natural world are not limited to Brazilian rainforests. His arguments fall largely on deaf ears, he's sure, but he continues to make them because, after years of repeating himself, it's easier to continue than to stop.

He and Ruby have not seen their oldest son for more than three years. He left, years ago, under cloudy skies. By that point he had been arrested half a dozen times for half a dozen reasons that did not include drugs and for that his parents were grateful. He had stolen cars, among other things, but he denied his involvement in many of the forcible break-ins of which he stood accused. And since he made such half-hearted efforts to conceal the robberies he did commit, his parents began, despite themselves, to trust him.

Ruby says, Do you think Tom is all right, I hope he's all right. Archie says nothing, because he doesn't have an answer, and because he knows that Ruby doesn't expect one. She just needs to say certain things now and again, and so he waits for what seems a reasonable period of time before he changes the subject.

3

When Archie said, How would you feel if I planted a tree in the living room? Ruby held her breath. She knew that one of two things was going to happen and neither depended on her. Archie was either going to correct himself and acknowledge that this idea of his was a bad one, or he was going to walk into the garage where his tools were. She waited and was about to tell him that she also thought that trees were best kept out of doors, in nature, but she misjudged his pause. He said, after a deep breath, that he should dig first. So he began, making quick work of the living room, an admittedly underused corner of the house, but one that has been, for several years now, just the way Ruby wanted it.

So, while Archie set to work inside, Ruby got her own tools together and went to the garden. She's had two or three good weeks of summer already and the heat has stayed down. The perennials have made a good showing. Some, in fact, bloomed early and have held on later than she's seen in years. She cuts these close to the soil and moves them indoors where vases are waiting. She digs up a few bulbs to transplant, adds a new layer of soil, smooths it flat with an open palm.

Christopher has not weeded as thoroughly as he assured her he had. She expected as much but is still going to let him hear about it. She says, Why did I find so many weeds in the yard this morning? Christopher says that he must have pulled a thousand yesterday and that he's sorry. He says, You can't expect me to get them all. Archie says that it's human perception that determines what is and is not a weed and that it's unfortunate we're so determined, as a society, to banish anything we don't deem useful. There are some lovely weeds after all, he says, many even flower. The grass we mow is a weed, let's not forget that. This gives Christopher a little support, it seems. That's right, he says. Who are we to say? To this, Ruby says that no one wants to buy a weed, which is where that particular conversation finds its conclusion. Then she looks through the kitchen window for a long time as Delores and Archie work on their sandwiches and as Christopher sets to work on an enormous bowl of cereal. Ruby says, I hope Tom is all right. She turns to see that Delores is watching her, and that she has a sad look in her eye. Ruby asks about Dale and how late he stayed last night. Delores explains that Dale wishes she could yodel because he thinks a yodeler is really what his band needs right now. No offense or anything, Delores says, mimicking Dale's voice, but the saw is just so sad. She makes air quotes with the fingers on the one hand that still has them. He wants a new banjo player, Delores says, like he needs another one.

In the garden, Ruby is a master. She can manage to keep every bed in bloom from spring to early winter, and she's managed to make a name for herself as an expert on all things botanical. For her crops and her classes, and more recently for her arrangements, she's featured each year in several local publications. The flowers she sells are not exclusively or even mostly the flowers she grows (fresh cuts shipped in daily), but her personal garden is no small testament to her hard work.

What amazes Ruby most is how easily weeds reproduce themselves. Why can't the flowers grow so well, and seed so efficiently? She has admitted, on more than one occasion, that she's much less likely to enjoy a garden that has not been manicured and shaped by human hands. Which is to say that she's not inclined to keep volunteer trees or a bed of wildflowers. Wildflowers are nice, she doesn't want to be misunderstood, but they're meant for the wild, for nature. No garden is natural, she says, any more than the clothes she wears or the food she eats. These things have been touched by human hands and have ceased, therefore, to be natural. Why would she try to convince herself otherwise? Everything started at some point in nature, that much is clear, but let's not be lazy about this whole thing. Ultimately, Ruby says, she's just too proud to take credit for any bed of flowers that would have grown just as well without her.

Ruby heard Delores talking to Dale. She heard Delores say that she was not so interested, as she once might have been, in Honky Tonk, that she was not as enamored as she used to be. She didn't want Dale to get the wrong idea, she said, but she's not the same person she once was. Dale said that he needed Delores to be strong right now and that being strong meant being consistent, and that meant she should try to find what mattered most to her. It sounded to Ruby like Dale was trying to tell Delores what should matter most to her, which is no surprise. Ruby has not been fond of Dale from the get-go and her opinion has not changed since Delores had her accident.

Maybe you should make a clean start, Ruby says later. Maybe you should find a way to wipe the slate clean. She may be saying too much, and her plan might backfire, but she's already weighed the risk against the benefit. She doesn't want to be misunderstood, but it's not a bad idea to begin again. There will be other boys. There will be other reasons to go out on a Friday night. Yes, Delores says, I guess there will be. But she doesn't think making a clean start is as easy as her mother says it can be. There are questions to be asked and there are answers and maybe she needs to be patient. Ruby may have said too much.

The saw is such an interesting instrument, Ruby tells Delores. Did she know that some people play the garden hose like a French horn? Yes, Delores has seen such things. Delores is quick to remind her mother that she's not playing the saw because it's unique or unusual. She's playing it, she says, because no other instrument can manage to produce a sound so haunting and ethereal. The saw, she says, is not a substitute. It's not a stand-in for something else, but the genuine article. She plays the saw because that's what she does, and she wouldn't have it any other way.

It's true that certain music dictionaries have been quick to dismiss the saw as a novelty even if they afforded it an illustrated entry in many cases. They poke fun, but so what? Besides, the saw is no easy thing to play. Sure, just about anybody can make the saw sound a note or two, it takes hardly any effort, but has she considered, Delores asks her mother, that for all the respect it gets as a serious instrument, any infant can play a note on a piano? A cat can do it, for that matter. To really make music with the saw is no easier than to do the same with a piano. Delores knows enough about other instruments, she says, and she knows that the saw is harder to play, by a mile, than a guitar. So what if it didn't take a craftsman in Vienna a decade to produce her instrument? So what if the best examples are those you can find at any hardware store? Does difficulty in the production of an instrument have anything to do, really, with the quality of its playing? Let's be honest, Delores says. Let's be honest and admit that there's no other instrument that can play a song and then cut down a tree and then play another song. Ruby has to give it to her there, she can't name one. She wouldn't mind using Delores's instrument to do some cutting herself, she says. Delores laughs, and Ruby says, Well, it's much later than I thought.

4

When his sister chopped off her fingers, Christopher knew something important had happened. Not something good important, but something big important. This was not something that would fade quickly into the background he knew, even then. He felt guilty at first for his interest in seeing his sister's hand. He knew that he couldn't just come out and stare at the thing or inspect it very closely, but he was as curious as he could imagine being and he couldn't help it if he was.

Her hand, once he caught a reasonable glimpse, didn't look so strange. He was disappointed, of course, that it looked so normal, so common, and so much like any hand with its fingers folded down on themselves. Even he could make his hand look fingerless from the right angles. If Delores's hand looked fingerless—was fingerless—from every angle, it didn't really matter since he could see only one angle at a time and that one angle didn't look so bizarre. He had questions, of course. Did it hurt? Was there sensation in the nubs? Did she wake to feel an itch or a tickle? She answered his questions until their mother told him to knock it off. Delores was a good sport.

Christopher feeds crickets to the various rodents he keeps in his room. He watches them eat up; he watches them hide themselves away again. He's realized, though, that maybe his interest in rodents and reptiles is not what it once was. He's kept his aquariums full of various and assorted pets for so long that he has trouble remembering anything else, but maybe he's outgrowing his interest in pets that can't be trusted to run freely in the house. His friends have dogs and cats, and they seem fine. He likes dogs especially because of their willingness to play games. Although the eating habits of his snakes are interesting and complex, he finds that as companions the snakes are less than stimulating company. A dog, he thinks, is what he will get next, after his current set of pets have died or been set free. He wonders what his mother will think if he sets any of these creatures loose in the yard or near the greenhouses.

Christopher finds himself less willing to abandon the enormous ant farm that sits along the far wall of his bedroom. He built this Plexiglas experiment with his father's help, and it's been more than adequate for the hundreds of ants who have made a home of it. While the snakes and toads and mice have begun to seem less interesting to him, the ants have caught his attention like never before. There's a section of the ant farm that serves as a starting point, a point from which every other point is down, but once his ants have moved below that point, through one of the two entrances to their tunnels, they enter an elaborate and complicated network that wraps around itself like a maze. That all these pathways are consistent and well used speaks to the sort of efficiency he's come to admire. They waste nothing, these ants, and more than that, they keep their world in perfect order. Though a pathway might occasionally collapse (if Christopher is a god, he's an active one), he's always amazed by the speed and efficiency of repair efforts or the construction of alternate routes. What amazes him most is that the ants work so hard but seem to accomplish so little. Their paths produce a fantastic pattern, and the ants move around themselves so fluidly, but in the end, Christopher sees that for all their effort they have accomplished nothing. They work because it's what they do and sometimes he pities them for it.

In his father's biology class Christopher finds himself uncomfortable with the questions his father asks. He doesn't say penis at home with any frequency, so why is he obligated to do so here? Everyone knows the word and they don't need his dad to remind them of it. Get used to it, Archie says, and Christopher realizes that he might need to get used to a few things.

When Archie assigns a project to the class, Christopher doesn't take notes. He'll get around to collecting seeds sooner or later. How hard could it be? Right now, his only concern is the fifteen minutes he has to endure until the bell rings, and he's set free. Archie shows some mercy and doesn't call on Christopher to name any of the places one might find seeds or where one might look to identify a specific tree by name. Christopher is thankful, in small ways, that his father recognizes how uncomfortable this is for him. He also knows that a good place to find seeds is in his house, where a small tree has recently been planted. He doesn't share this information with his classmates because he knows that they care about trees no more than he does.

And speaking of weeds, Ruby says. Christopher has heard this tone before. He knows that his mother is not happy with his work in the backyard. It isn't because his work was lacking but because she needs something to complain about. Ruby says, And speaking of weeds, I found so many in the beds this morning. Christopher says, I got most of them. This is where his father chimes in with some speech about weeds and having a positive approach to nature. We must accept that nature is not dependent on our perceptions of beauty. A weed, Archie is saying, is only another kind of flower, a beautiful grass, and we shouldn't be so quick to banish them. Not that we stand a chance of doing so even if we try. That's right, Christopher says, who are we to say what a weed is? Besides, he thinks, there's no way he could have pulled them all. Ruby says that if she can't sell it, it's a weed and Christopher sees that he'll make no headway with her today.

He pours himself a bowl of cereal and ducks behind the box, staring at a maze he finds there, a maze so easily solved that he has trouble working his way to even one of the dead ends. He wonders who could possibly find this sort of thing challenging. His ants have done better.

Ruby says, I hope Tom is all right, and Archie just stares back at her. Delores puts her sandwich down and pushes herself from the table with the palms of both hands. Christopher sees, as well as he has ever seen, the smooth, rounded flesh where fingers used to be.

The Future King

The heavyset man doesn't want to imagine the guillotine, or the power he has to send a man or woman to his or her death, or the perverse irony just waiting for any king who might do so. The irony hangs in the air, heavy and sharp, as he sits and thinks beneath the unnerving weight of his crown and kingdom. Despite his efforts, the heavyset man does find that his thoughts sometimes drift in the direction of the guillotine. It's such an efficient machine. He finds it easy to admire the near total perfection of its design. Though he admits it to no one, the heavyset man—quite unintentionally—finds himself imagining the queen kneeling before that great machine, waiting pleasantly for the end of things. Why this awful thought, he doesn't know. After all, he loves the queen. Loves her the way a king ought to love a queen, as much as any kind, virtuous, benevolent king can and should love his regal counterpart.

He would like something other than tapestries. He would like other kings to stop with these gifts. What he would prefer is a good all-weather, double-paned window for his bedchamber. What he would like even more is a relatively simple duct system through which air, conditioned against the natural temperature and humidity, could flow into his living space. In fact, he would like a number of things that haven't been invented. He keeps himself awake at night making lists of such things. In his bed, the heavyset man finds himself too hot or too cold, the air too dry or too heavy with moisture. He imagines solutions that haven't yet been considered, not by anyone, not ever. He takes some small pleasure in these concoctions of his mind, these formulations and mechanisms.

He's in love with a young woman who isn't his wife, or slightly in love with her. He knows that the world is filled with queens, both near and far, and that this young woman is not among them, but he also knows that new queens are everywhere, just waiting to happen. He forces himself to think of anything else: the manufacture of boiled leather, the weight of a castle wall, the upkeep of stables. Still, he sometimes feels helpless to control his thoughts which settle on that young woman upon whom he has the slightest, most inappropriate, most un-kingly crush. That woman who is fully clothed head to foot and yet seems, strangely, unpredictably, illogically to be wearing nothing at all. It's her special privilege, he believes, to exist as a beautiful, chaste, fully clothed young woman and to somehow seem like something else. She has about her a modest immodesty. It's a small trick she has, a sleight of hand. What is it, he wonders, about this woman that so draws his attention?

He knows that there are, have been, will be many kings in the world. He knows, too, that the world, in all its vastness, is not so vast. He knows that there will always be more men who want to be king than men who can be king. That is to say that the world is filled with threats upon threats and a king really ought to watch his back. There are only so many pretenders and uprisers and deceivers one can store away in the royal dungeon, only so many one can place beneath the guillotine. Only so many aspirants one can remove through war and counter-deceit and cleverly considered bits of espionage.

And the threats don't end with men who want to be king. There are just as many queens who wouldn't mind taking control of things for a while. Yes, there are would-be kings and would-be queens and peasants with pitchforks and flames and secret manipulations of the water supply. He won't allow himself to forget poisoned darts and poisoned arrows, poisoned wine in poisoned goblets, drops of poison dropped gently into the sleeping ear, poisoned fowl and poisoned game at a poisoned table, poisoned knives in the back and poisoned knives in the front.

Isn't it true that he is, as king, in a unique position? Isn't it true that he, of all people, has the right to know as much as anyone knows? Isn't it true that he ought to be the one in possession of every piece of knowledge available in his kingdom? Isn't his court filled with doctors and scientists and bookish men whose knowledge is his to retrieve when the time is appropriate for retrieval? Isn't it true that certain combinations of things, plant and animal extracts, minerals, rare fluids and elements, might be mixed and compounded into other things that are, somewhat magically, greater than the sum of their parts? Isn't it true that certain alchemical concoctions have the power to cure a man just as easily as they might blind, hobble, or kill him? Isn't it true that certain members of his court have taken to whispering, claiming that they only meant to avoid disturbance? Isn't it true that the heavyset man's wife, the queen, has, of late, taken a peculiar interest in an herb garden she planted on the roof of a distant, hard-to-locate tower in some rarely used quarter of the castle? Isn't it true that the kingdom has become, of late, a place absolutely bursting with vials and glasses and goblets holding oddly colored, strangely cool, vaguely cloudy substances? Hasn't he, the heavyset man, been invited to try them all, to finish off these concoctions, each presented as an ale or a wine or a cure for dyspepsia? Hasn't he demurred?

Haven't his excuses run thin? Haven't his worries, doubts, and skepticisms become increasingly obvious? Hasn't he been left with nothing but mistrust of his unloyal ones, his unloving ones, his deceitful kith and kin?

As disguises go, this is a good one. After all, he's completely covered, head to foot. Or nearly so. He's covered well enough to know that the people haven't grown wise. To them, he's merely an old person hobbling through the mucky, muddy street. What would they think, or do, or say if they knew that he, their king, was out among them? Would this be good news? Would it intimidate them and cause distress? Would they imagine that he, their benevolent king, was up to something? Would they accept the possibility that he was only curious about the daily lives and work of his people? Would they accept this as a sociological study of the daily lives of the toiling class, the impoverished, muck-dwelling, tax-paying, farm-tilling people? It seems unlikely that he could reveal himself and not cause confusion and agitation, so he keeps hidden beneath his oversized cloak. Hunched over like this, hobbling like this, he does a decent job imitating the walking behavior of a very old person, although he admits that there are very few old people in his kingdom, being, as this is, an age in which people do not often live beyond a few short decades. This will change in the distant future, as life expectancy doubles and then doubles again. If he's too large a man to reasonably pass for a starving peasant, and if his cloak is of too fine a fabric, and if his shimmering shoes—gifts from exotic realms far to the east—are too ornate, he hopes that the overall effect is enough to convince his people. He hears nothing of interest as he stops and leans heavily on wooden fences, beams, and stanchions. He hears only the muffled sounds of farm animals lowing, the sounds of his kingdom in motion. He would like to throw back his hood, throw off his cloak. He would like to stand atop some table and reveal himself and announce loudly that he knows about the plots and plans and schemes of this toiling class. He would show them how fully he's infiltrated their ranks and has discovered their revolt in the making: their nascent revolution, their early plot to topple the king and his court, to storm the castle, to wrest power from those who hold it. But he has no data just yet, no useful evidence that he can possibly use to show that he knows what he claims to know.

The woman he loves he loves more each day. He knows that her condition is not one that merely happens, as though by sorcery, as though by a nudge from the fates, but that there's a mechanics to the thing: a consequence for every deed. He watches her, sees that her face is flush, her breathing labored, her beautiful belly ever so slightly larger than it was yesterday, last week, last month. He knows further, and to his great disappointment, that he has had no part in this chain of events. He would like to say something, to hint that he knows. And why not? Certainly not because he lacks the privilege, right, or power to say and do as he feels. It's only because he's a more tactful man than that, a more refined, discrete, judicious man than that. He says nothing. What good might come of words? What can he possibly do but sit and watch and know that somewhere not far from here is a luckier man than he? He's left only with this brief opportunity to serve as witness to her illness, condition, state. It's a state he finds mirrored by his wife, the queen. She's less flushed, perhaps, and breathes more easily, but isn't there still the evidence, a protrusion or bump? Isn't this good news? Isn't this a thing he has wished for, pined for? Good news, yes, because what's a king without heir, father without son, quiver without arrow? What's he to do with his largely empty castle, his hundreds, thousands, millions of rooms, mile after mile of unexplored square footage?

Given the hypothetical option to travel through time and, given the hypothetical conditions that one must choose to travel only forward or only backward and that one must travel only once and not multiple times, the heavyset man decides that he would much prefer to travel forward in time. Given the choice he would most likely opt for a jump of several centuries of time in his all-at-once adventure. His reasoning for this is simple. First, he knows that the future is more interesting than the past, given that the future contains what is already past and what is not yet past but will be the past before the future arrives, while the past contains only the past and, more importantly, an even smaller portion of the past than the one he currently has to work with. Second, although he knows a great many things, he's skeptical about transferable knowledge. He wonders, that is, what he could possibly offer to people in the past that would be of value to them while he knows that what he knows would be of great value to people of the future who likely know much more than he knows even though they remain, figuratively, in the dark when it comes to knowing his particular mind regarding certain decisions he made, representing, as he does, not only himself, but all kings, rulers, monarchs of his historical moment. The people of the future may want to know, that is, why he made this decision or that one, why he invaded this kingdom or that one, why he beheaded this person or that one. Third, he suspects that a return trip from the future, assuming that such a return was part of the agreed-upon conditions of time travel, would increase his power as king. It would, at the very least, allow him to seem, to future generations, a man of even greater knowledge than he already is or seems. Given no choice and given the obligation to travel backward in time or not at all, the heavyset man decides that he would likely travel only a brief distance in time, maybe only a month, or a week, or a couple of days. He imagines the things he might do, the plots he might undo, the schemes he might undermine if he were able to reverse time only briefly, in such a limited way.

The Keeper of the Seal says only that he wants to know the whereabouts of His Grace at all times. Sire, he says, it is for your safety. Yes, the heavyset man says, I understand completely. He does understand, although he wouldn't mind understanding a little better, why the Keeper of the Seal needs to know what he says he needs to know. All this *where will you be* and *where are you going* and *when should we expect your departure* and so on. It's a little dizzying, quite frankly, and the heavyset man says that he isn't always sure and can't always be expected to be sure where he'll be and when he'll be there. The Keeper of the Seal says that the king of the people ought to be careful and cautious and more completely in control of the situations he puts himself in. The Keeper of the Seal says that the king might indulge his every whim but that for his own safety he ought to limit the variables. The heavyset man isn't certain which variables the Keeper of the Seal refers to and which variables he doesn't, so he tries a little test. When the Keeper of the Seal asks where the king intends to be tomorrow, after he has supped and before he retires, the heavyset man proceeds to tell the Keeper of the Seal where he was last night during that same window of time. Yes, yes, the Keeper of the Seal says, but tomorrow, where will you be tomorrow? The heavyset man brushes this question off and says that on the day after tomorrow, during that same window of time, he intends to visit the stables to see how things go with his hundreds of horses, his thousands of horses, his horses without number. This, of course, sends the Keeper of the Seal into a small, barely concealed fit. Yes, he says, that's all fine and good, but I have asked you about tomorrow. Oh, tomorrow? The heavyset man says. Well, I haven't really thought through my schedule for tomorrow. I might be anywhere during that window of time tomorrow.

Tell me, why do you ask? The Keeper of the Seal, visibly agitated, says again that it's all for the safety of the king. Yes, thank you, says the heavyset man. I'll let you know when I settle my agenda. As the Keeper of the Seal slinks off to wherever it is he goes, the heavyset man wonders if he is, in fact, the first person in the history of the world to refer to a window of time. The phrase gives him a strange pleasure.

The heavyset man knows that his vast-but-somehow-still-limited world is filled with unclean things. He knows that a cough might soon become something worse, that a bruise might portend some greater misfortune, that any cut or scrape might be all it takes to set one on a short path to the grave. He knows that his people live as cleanly as they can but that they're limited by certain facts and obligations. If they prepare food and eat it only a stone's throw from where their pigs and goats and cows eat, sleep, and defecate, it is not because they believe it to be a good idea. It is, rather, because they have no choice and do the best they can. It is, he knows, because a stone's throw is the greatest distance they can put between their food and the infected waste of their farm animals. What other option do they have? He admires his people and their knack for not dying more often than they do. He wouldn't mind rewarding their ingenuity and relative longevity, but how and in what way? Giving them land is bad policy, as it takes from them a necessary sense of subjugation, because you give an inch and then what, where does it end? But they're resilient, these people, living well into their third or fourth decade sometimes. This is good. This is proof of something. The heavyset man knows it isn't unreasonable for anyone to die at any time. The reasons for dying, the explanations offered by doctors and alchemists and mystics, is that this is simply the nature of things. Or that it's a problem in the stars. Or that the humors are out of balance. They never say that illness and death might be avoided if conditions were to become favorable to something other than illness and death. They don't say that maybe someone should invent penicillin or sterile bandages or refrigeration. They claim no responsibility. They say only that a woman with child is as likely as anyone to die too soon. They say only that the beautiful, chaste woman who used to empty his bedpan is now dead, and her child with her. All for nothing.

He has felt, at times, a genuine fondness for his queen and has believed her to be on his side. He's young and she's younger, and they've been married longer than they were ever not married. It's longer still if he counts those years of betrothal when he was still only a potential king and she a potential queen. He knows that such is the way with kingdoms. His is not a life in which one makes decisions based on anything other than the growth or continued control of the domain. A king is an idea and he's merely the current, physical embodiment of that idea. After him, there will be another and then another. He's not the king so much as the current occupant of a position that constitutes part of the kingdom. There's a kingliness to him. There's something appropriately royal about the way he moves, speaks, eats, but these are only learned behaviors. His wife, by extension, is the most recent manifestation of queenship. She's a queen because her father and his father agreed that this merger made good sense, economically and politically, but she's an ugly woman. Even if she were the most beautiful person in the entire, enormous, uncountably large kingdom, she would remain the ugliest person he knows. That ugliness runs deep in her bones and it sends a little shiver through him each time he sees her there across the full length of the dining hall, or when he sees her jawing at a servant for some impossibly small oversight, or when he sees her, more and more frequently, whispering something into the ear of the Keeper of the Seal. It's just as ugly the way the Keeper of the Seal smiles before turning to whisper something into that queenly ear. She laughs, too, and it's a filthy little laugh.

His queenly wife is not dead and not dying. She's the picture of health, the very manifestation of a vibrant, expectant woman. Her cheeks, puffy and red, announce that she has, of course, taken on a little weight, but otherwise there's little evidence of change. In fact, he wonders to what extent the members of his court are fully aware that he is soon to be the father to a child, the next king or queen. That is, if all goes well, if the tides don't shift. He wonders if these, his closest and most trusted ones, his dearest advisers, his coterie of inside men, know that he is about to become something different than what he has been. Will they clap in delight? Will they accept this information as a given, as an obvious extension of what they already know? Will they nod their official heads and say official things? The heavyset man wonders how his court will feel about this new situation. He wonders why it is that in the face of evidence that he's capable of producing an heir he feels so melancholy. He wonders why this news is not the news he apparently wanted. What might he have preferred? What in the vast world could be better than to know that he has established a link to his own immortality?

It's a jewel-encrusted box filled with jewel-encrusted swords and jewel-encrusted shields. A gift from a small consortium of kings from a small conglomerate of kingdoms. They might as well be regents or viceroys the way they look to the heavyset man for what is right and appropriate. There are, too, helmets and bits of armor. These represent, in sum, the playthings of a child. This box with its jewels and playthings is a gift from kings who have received word, they say in their wax-sealed note, that he, this kingly king, is to be a father. This gift, they hope, will go some way toward assuring that the child is a boy and therefore a future king. This is only right, they write. This is the way it ought to be and should be and is to be. They say they're happy and delighted and filled with joy for the king and the queen and the forthcoming prince (fingers crossed). The heavyset man is also happy or should be happy. Why isn't he happier? He wonders why the news of an heir to the throne doesn't delight him the way he always thought it would. He wonders why he feels only disdain for his wife, the queen. Is this the thing he wanted or something false? He wonders how the other kings got word, and so soon, about the as-yet-unborn child. He wonders how it's possible that they should know so soon after his own discovery. Does this mean, he wonders, that word was sent to the other kings before he received word himself? Does this mean that even now the queen and the Keeper of the Seal and his various advisors and confidantes are circulating news and information? Is he so far removed from the inner workings of his own kingdom? He has to wonder about that jewel-encrusted sword, that plaything. Isn't it a weapon? Isn't the gift of a weapon to a child an invitation for bloodshed? Isn't this evidence enough that his son, his unborn heir, is already plotting, plotting without the capacity to plot, plotting by virtue of the plot plotted for him, the death of his father, the king? He will die someday and some other will rule in his place. He doesn't want to believe this and resists thinking the thought, but it's one he can't avoid. He'll die young because the odds dictate that he must. He knows that his wife is a factory for future despots. He knows that the world, his kingdom, is filled with so many grabby hands, each pair content with nothing less than everything.

At the Gates of the Kingdom

The first door was taller than seemed necessary. It was eight feet, at least, but narrow. It was made of heavy, dark wood, perhaps rosewood or walnut. It was also ornately carved, and I couldn't help but think of it as an altarpiece. There was nothing on it to suggest it belonged in a church, but it was clearly the result of great effort. If I'm honest, I tend to think of churches in that way, as places built by long work. The door consisted of four main panels and each panel was twice inlaid, giving the appearance of windows within windows. Both in and around the four panels, the wood was covered by leaf and vine patterns, as though the whole thing were covered in ivy. There was no portion of the door that was flat or smooth and I suspected that knocking would achieve little, except perhaps to bloody my knuckles. I still tried to knock, using the fleshy side of my fist, but I felt as though the door swallowed up any sound I created. It was clearly not a door for knocking. I looked for a bell or an intercom but found nothing.

It was a cool, gusty day. It had been hot for a week or more, and the sudden shift toward coolness caught me off guard. I had dressed for a different kind of weather, and I found the erratic bursts of wind were making me irritable. I stood there for a few moments, considering whether and where I might try again to knock, looking for a space that provided the greatest hope of producing a useful sound when I noticed that the door was not closed tight. In fact, I could see a good portion of the strike plate inside the door's frame. I gave a little push then and found the door to be heavier than I expected. It gave some ground, slowly at first, but then more easily. Finally, as its hinges began to bear the full weight of the door, it seemed to slide away from me, opening itself. It came to rest, quite naturally, in a fully open position. As I crossed through the doorway, I couldn't help but think of Hawthorne's poor Wakefield and how the threshold represents not only the entrance to a home, but also the decision to participate in a system, or rather, the end of the refusal to participate in a system. A door in that sense is a kind of rejection, and I found the idea intriguing.

I only had space for a step or two before I came to the second door. It was also made of heavy wood, but with much less ornamentation. What caught my attention more fully, though, was the way this door seemed weather worn. The wood here—much lighter in tone, perhaps white oak— appeared to have taken the full effect of many years' exposure to the elements. The bottom inches of the door showed clear evidence of water damage, and the whole thing, while clearly preserved to some degree, showed cracking and splintering that only comes from extended exposure to sun and wind and rain. Looking around, I could see that I had not entered the building in earnest just yet, but that I was standing instead in a kind of anteroom. Why anyone would build such an addition was beyond me, and especially so considering the lack of any obvious use suggested by this space. I wondered if perhaps the room I was standing in might be some kind of coat room, but again the size of it suggested no such thing. What I could see, though, was that this addition to the building was relatively new. The brickwork of the addition stood out, if only just, in contrast to the older brickwork of what I took to be the original building. The mortar, too, showed a distinction. For whatever reason, someone had thought to extend the building in this very small way. It left me feeling that I was both inside and outside the building at once. It was a strange sensation.

There was a doorbell button to the right of the door. It was the sort that ought to be illuminated, but this one was not. I figured its bulb had burned out. I pushed the button and listened closely for the report of a bell or chime on the other side of the door. Hearing nothing, I waited for half a minute or so, knowing that a bell might very well have sounded without my hearing it, but nothing happened and no one responded. I pushed the button again and waited again. I repeated this process maybe five or six times. Each time I pushed the button I felt a small, illogical burst of pleasure. It was pointless, of course, but I liked pushing that button and waiting. The button gave a satisfying resistance and gave me the sense of actively doing something. This is a hard thing for me to describe, but I often long for a physical response to things I've done. I'm told it has something to do with what are called mechanoreceptors and the body's desire for tactile feedback, but what I know for sure is that I have felt an increasing anxiety over the past decades. Computers and computer-like devices might do a great many things, but they too often fail to give clear evidence of received input. With computers there's always that helpless waiting, a period in which one must consider that perhaps the waiting is in vain. The thinking a computer does is complex, but I long for simple things done clearly and cleanly. It's ironic, I know, to lament the feedback a computer won't give as I reflect on a doorbell that seemed not to work at all, but still, in that moment I felt tangible satisfaction each time I pushed that button. I might have stayed there and pushed it all day long.

Eventually, the second door did open, although at first I could see no one standing there to answer it, and I assumed that this door, like the first, was weighted so as to open itself. I thought about ghosts for a moment and entertained the notion, however ridiculous, that this building was haunted and that some specter had opened the door to greet me. I liked to imagine that kind of thing from time to time if only for the pleasure of exercising the imagination, but I also found that such thinking inevitably led to disappointment. And that's exactly what happened now as I leaned in through the doorway. What I saw there was no ghost, just a short man in a brown suit. He was distinctive only in the way we all are. His features, taken separately, were very much like others I had come to know well. I recognized his nose (too large for his face), his white eyebrows (in need of a trim), his weak chin, and a slight redness in his cheeks. I had never seen the man before, but I was disappointed by his ordinariness. He didn't smile or seem to think much of me, and it seemed possible that he hadn't opened the door for me at all, that maybe he had opened the door for some other reason. He stood there and simply watched for a moment, as though waiting for me to declare my intentions. Before I could say anything, though, he invited me to come in. Please, he said, and made that hand-across-body gesture that makes us all look like bullfighters. The room I now entered was scarcely larger than the one I had just been in, but this one felt distinctly like the inside of something. The lighting here was very dim and I felt for a moment that I had traveled back in time to a candle-lit parlor or drawing room. I was just noticing how very low the ceiling in this room was when the man in the brown suit asked that I excuse him. I nodded and he left the room. He left by the same door I had just entered, which struck me as odd but also served as proof that he hadn't opened the door for me at all. He'd opened it for himself. I had assumed him to be some kind of butler or concierge, but now I realized that I didn't know who or what he was. I guessed that he might return at any moment, but I never saw him again.

There was, in that room, a small wooden bench and very little else. The light came from a single lamp on the wall—a sconce, I guess—and the illumination it produced came from a weak, low-wattage bulb. There were two doors: the one I had come through and another on the opposite wall. On the floor there was a small rug with an intricate serpentine pattern. I took it to be of indigenous design, but I knew little of such things and could have said no more than that. There was, in the corner, a large ceramic pot about three feet tall. It was empty, but I took it as an umbrella stand, which only solidified my suspicion that this room was the true entry to the building. If the room I had just left was an anteroom, it was only an anteroom to an anteroom.

I was reminded of my years at school and how we had, on occasion, found opportunity to slip away from our studies—or the appearance of studies—to explore the various corners of the old building. We rarely found anything on those excursions into janitorial closets and storage rooms, but we did, once, discover an unlocked utility closet, inside of which we found a ladder leading down into some maintenance tunnels. We were too young and too easily frightened to explore very far into those tunnels just then, and lamentably we never found the closet unlocked again. What we did find, though, on that first and only trip down the ladder, was a map of the school nailed to the wall just at the base of the ladder. The map looked something like a blueprint or a schematic, and it showed every room and every corridor in the entire building. It was hard for us to read the map since it abstracted and layered so much that was, to us, the very core of our dull and concrete daily reality. But we did find something there that captured our attention. In addition to the various classrooms and offices labeled on the map, we found that the area between the two sets of doors at the front of the building was labeled. This area—one we had never before paused to consider—was called the vestibule. It was a word we didn't know and it seemed to us somehow magical. It was a foolish thing, of course, to be so taken by an architectural label for something so common, but there we were, repeating the word to ourselves as though it were a practical incantation. That was the memory that came back to me in that small room. I was, I realized, in this building's vestibule.

I sat quietly for several long minutes, thinking about my schooldays. Before long I began to suspect that my waiting was pointless. No one, it seemed, was coming to find me, and I didn't assume I would cause any inconvenience by merely opening the door and calling out to anyone who might hear me. I decided to do just that. The third door was plain and sturdy looking and hardly called my attention, but the knob to that door was golden and as elegant as anything in the world. At first, I hesitated even to touch it. It was large— too much so, I thought—and it was every bit as ornate as the wood of the first door, but here I found more than vine and leaf. In the middle of the knob was an image of a dog. Initially, I mistook it for a lion, but the face was too thin and the hair too long, and at last I decided it was likely a hound of some sort, probably an Irish Setter. I had to admit that I didn't know if the Irish Setter was technically a hound, but I could do little to satisfy that question under the circumstances. What I knew was that it was not likely a lion and looked a great deal like the Irish Setter I had always wanted as a child. Around the image of the dog was a series of stars and harps that appeared to rest on latticework. The harps weren't distinctly Gaelic, but they might well have been the reason I took the animal for an Irish Setter in the first place.

I then began to wonder whether or not the Irish Setter was Irish in any way. I didn't know the answer to that question, but I did know that Bus Eireann used the Irish Setter for its logo, and this seemed about as close to a definitive answer as I could give myself. (I feel I should admit that at the time I had never been to Ireland.) I tried to turn the knob, but soon realized that it was not that type of mechanism. Instead, it was really only a handle by which to push or pull the door. I gave it a slight push and felt the door move open. I then entered a dark room that seemed as large and as empty as any I had ever known.

I say the room seemed large because it quickly became clear that it was not large at all. The room was only slightly larger than the vestibule, but there was something about the room, the quality of light there and the quality of the paint on the walls, that allowed shadows a great depth. Looking across the room, I had the sense I was looking across a great chasm or into a starless expanse of space. It took a few minutes for my eyes to make sense of the place in the low light before I realized just how empty this room was. There was nothing here. No furniture, nothing on the walls, and nothing on the floor. There was not, as far as I could tell, even crown molding on the walls. I heard once that it takes forty minutes for the human eye to adjust to darkness, and I considered that I might wait here as my eyes acclimated. Rods or cones, I knew, were doing their work, but I didn't know which was which. This room confused me for a number of reasons, but its primary trick was that seeming depth. Each time I turned around, I thought I could see the room stretching out in the distance before me, but almost as soon as I started off to explore, the room ended again. This happened several times and left me feeling both frustrated and confused. I seemed to be in a room with only one entrance, and yet it hardly made sense for a building so large to end so soon. If I had been disappointed by the man in the brown suit, I only felt a greater disappointment here. I couldn't make sense of this room, and I couldn't understand why I had been allowed to wait here so long. I don't know what I had expected, exactly, but this did not, as they say, fit the bill.

Eventually, as my eyes began to perceive more acutely, I did see something new. To my great relief, I noticed a long line running down the wall of the room opposite the door by which I entered. The line, when I inspected it, revealed itself to be a seam. When I put a little weight on the wall just there, a part of it gave way and opened. This fourth door wasn't a door, properly speaking, or if it was, it was a secret door. I felt a certain pride in myself just then, as though I were a detective and had just found the clue that would signal the end of a great mystery. I'm no expert on the topic of mystery novels, but I've read a few in my time. I've always best enjoyed detective novels and particularly those in which the detective is, to one degree or another, common. What I mean is that I have little patience for the great masterminds and geniuses. I take little pleasure in watching brilliance parade itself before me as though it were my job merely to observe and feel awe. I feel little inclination for Dupin, or Holmes, or even Marple. Instead, I like those books in which the detective finds him or herself looking at evidence that makes no sense, doesn't add up. I like, figuratively speaking, standing there next to those detectives, wondering with them about this random data that points nowhere at all. I like best of all those moments in which simple chance breaks a case open. It isn't genius that saves the day, but hard work and good fortune. Standing in that room, looking at the hidden doorway I had just discovered, I felt that I had found my clue. I pushed the fourth door open and saw a small light some thirty feet away. I was standing at the dark end of a narrow corridor.

I could see that the corridor ended with a door and that the light came from another small sconce just to its left. The walls seemed to belong to another century. Again, I had the sense that I had stepped back in time. The lower portions of the walls were wainscoted, while the upper portions were covered in ornate damask wallpaper. The paper was flocked velvet, and the damask pattern was deep blue or purple, while the negative space was a brilliant white. There were a series of three unlit sconces on each wall and between the sconces I found paintings of identical rectangular dimensions. Each painting was of a different hilly landscape, but they were sufficiently similar as to seem interchangeable. They were the kinds of paintings one might examine very closely and never find anything worthy of comment. I, for one, had nothing to say about them and walked quickly to the door. Given the qualities of this corridor, I was surprised to find that the fifth door was nothing more than a cheap hollow core. It seemed wrong, somehow, for this door to be in this corridor. I reached for the door and found it very cool to the touch. I stood there a moment and wondered if there was any reason to wait here. I turned and looked back at the paintings on the walls and wondered if they were important works and I had been too hasty to recognize them for what they were. That reminded me of an experience I once had at London's National Gallery. This was about twenty-five years earlier, and I was quite young then. I found myself in the gallery out of a sense of obligation. I wanted to appreciate the work all around me, but appreciation meant something different then, as though I needed only to cross certain items off a to-do list. It might be better to say that I wanted to perform appreciation, and I thought that being in a museum was all I had to do. I had no context for the art I saw that day, and no instinct for it. I roamed around for maybe three quarters of an hour, listening to strangers as they commented on things I didn't understand. I was nearly on the point of leaving when I stumbled upon something that arrested my attention in an entirely unexpected way. The painting hanging there was Manet's *The Execution of Maximilian*, a large piece that occupied its own wall. What captivated me was the painting's fragmentary form and its use of white empty space. The scene itself, a depiction of a firing squad in the act of execution, meant nothing to me as a representation of history, but I stood there a long time considering Manet's aesthetic choices. Why, I wondered, had he chosen to place the firing squad, their backs turned, in the very center of the canvas? Why did the canvas stop short of the frame? It seemed to me the most interesting commentary on the act of seeing that I had ever encountered. I wanted to look at the face of Maximilian in the very moment of his death, but the artist refused me that privilege. What's more, he refused it in the most deliberate way by providing room for that face but producing no image to fill it. I was fascinated, too, by the guard at the rear of the squad, the one whose uniform and posture suggested that he was not directly involved in the execution but stood outside it somehow. That guard was given his own section of canvas, next to, but clearly separate from the larger body of firing soldiers. The way this officer casually inspects his rifle struck me as another indication that Manet meant to refuse us our impulse to see what we most want to see. Instead of examining the crude details of a public execution, he forces us to see the commonness happening just near it. I stood there and thought about that painting for a long while and only eventually brought myself to read the interpretive placard hanging on the wall. I was surprised and more than a little disappointed to discover that the painting was not what I had thought it to be. The fragmentation and empty space I saw there, the placard told me, were not part of the artist's conception, but were instead what they more obviously appeared to be. This painting, the first of several Manet would make on the subject of Maximilian's execution, had once been whole. What I saw before me was the best attempt to cobble together pieces from that original. Although Manet himself may have been responsible for cutting up that original canvas, I was troubled to think that what I admired so much was something of a flaw that others had worked hard to repair. I suppose my experience is similar to that of any child who might wonder why the Greeks sculpted all those armless women. I left the gallery that day feeling defeated. It was as though I had failed by liking what I should not. I turned back to the hollow core door, turned its cheap brass-plated handle, and let myself into the next room.

Or perhaps it would be better to say that I let myself out of the previous room since the room I now entered was no room at all. What I had entered was a large, rectangular area with brick walls on all sides and mosaic tile flooring. The walls rose high above me and finally disappeared into the star-filled darkness of the night sky. It was cold here and I had, for the second time, the distinct sense that I was both inside and outside at once. The air felt fresh and moved more calmly than it had before I entered the building. To be inside and outside at the same time is a strange feeling. If I had had some version of this experience when I first entered the building, I realized that it paled next to this. When I first entered the building, I might have turned to leave with a single step, but now I had the sense of being deep in the heart of something, with a long distance between me and the freedom of the outside world. What a strange sensation that was, to suddenly see myself as a kind of prisoner. There were no guards here and nothing to suggest that I was held against my will. There was not, in fact, anything to suggest that anyone even knew I was here. Anyone, that is, but a small man in a brown suit, but I didn't think it likely that he was out there locking doors behind me. There was only the sense of being in a position to see the outside world while being unable to move toward it. Then something else struck me. The sky I saw when I looked up didn't match the one I should have expected. It was the middle of the afternoon when I first entered the building, but now I was looking at a moonless night sky that was as dark as any could be. Many hours would have passed between then and now, but I was sure it had only been a matter of a few minutes, an hour at most, since I walked through that first door. How was I to explain this? I ran through a series of possibilities, each more implausible than the last, until I finally determined that what I was seeing was not the night sky, but a clever reproduction of it. I had seen such things before, in theaters and such, and I thought it impressive that someone had managed such a trick here. But no sooner had I put myself at ease that way than I saw a dark patch passing over the starry expanse above me. There appeared to be clouds up there, and I wondered whether I was looking at the real sky or a false one so convincing that it might have been preferable. I suddenly felt unsure about everything. By this point, my neck was beginning to ache, and I stopped looking at the sky or the reproduction of the sky. It was only then that I noticed what should have been obvious to me from the start.

The sixth door was made of long wooden slats, as if it belonged to a country fence. It was squared at the bottom, but curved at the top. The door was painted a turquoise blue and the paint had faded and cracked in many places. Through the slats and around the edges of the door, I could see evidence of a strong light. The light was not enough to illuminate the courtyard (or prison) I stood in, but it was bright enough to suggest some powerful light source on the other side. I approached the door cautiously, worried for the first time that I might disturb someone. I knocked lightly on the door and took a step back. I waited a few moments and then knocked again. It's hard for me to describe the sense of anxiety and anticipation I felt just then. It was a fear of that door, but also an overpowering desire to open it and rush through. I knocked several more times without answer. I found, before long, that I was pounding on the thing and began to fear I might damage it. I heard a sound then, like the whispered chirping of birds in a nest. I put my ear to the door and heard nothing. Then I realized the chirping was what it seemed, and that birds were above me, probably just outside my field of vision. That recognition sent a chill through me, though I can't say why exactly. I suspect it had something to do with my indecision about the nature of the sky. I decided I had waited long enough and pulled the door open.

What I discovered there was not at all what I expected. The light coming through the door was nowhere near as bright as I had thought (or hoped). It came from a single light bulb mounted to the door itself by a mechanic's clamp. A long extension cord ran from the light down the door and across the tiled floor until it disappeared beneath the wall. The bulb was blindingly bright, but I had expected something more. The room itself, which I expected for some reason to be cavernous, was quite small. To walk into it I was going to have to squat down a foot or so. I felt as though I were walking into a broom closet and this gave me no pleasure. I had little choice, though, and so I stepped through and found the room too dark to see in. With the door open, the bulb was now illuminating the courtyard/prison I had just been in, and if I was going to see anything I was going to need that bulb in here. I tried at first to simply pull the mechanic's clamp from the door, but it was secured, though I can't say how, well enough to escape my best effort. All I could do now was to bring the door closed behind me. And I did so.

Once illuminated, the room seemed both larger and more miserable than I thought. The ceiling rose as it moved away from the door I had just closed and allowed me to stand at full height after taking just a few steps in. The walls here were covered in soot and grime and I began to fear that I was breathing in mold spores. This had been a fear of mine for several years. I had watched a television program about a man who attempted to remove mold from beneath his house. Despite the man's best efforts to protect his lungs with a respirator, he was dead within days. I'm not the kind to live in fear of such things, but for one reason or another, the idea of molds and mycotoxins stayed with me. I felt that fear welling up now and wanted to move on as quickly as I could. There was a door here, a heavy iron thing. This seventh door struck me as the heaviest thing I had ever seen. The door's handle appeared to be a complicated mechanism at first, but I soon saw that it was quite simple. I tried the handle, but the door wouldn't open. I sat there and stared at the door for a few minutes before realizing that the complication of it was some kind of exposed locking mechanism and the door was almost certainly locked. But if it was locked, I noticed, I seemed to be on the inside of it. I looked and looked at the thing, finding nothing to pull on or turn. The only thing I could do, I guessed, was to pound on the door and hope that someone might open it for me. I had had, to this point, relatively little success with knocking, but I gave it a try, pounding again with the side of my fist rather than with my knuckles. The sound that came back to me was hollow and empty and I doubted that it carried very far at all. I tried the door again and realized that it was never going to open that way. Despite my fear of mold and because of the exhaustion that was beginning to come over me, I leaned my back against the wall and let my body slide down it until I was sitting on the floor. I wasn't sure what to do at this point. Having come this far, it seemed foolish to simply turn around and leave the way I had entered, but this seemed the only option. It really was a very strange building, I thought, the way room led on to room in such a linear fashion. I must have spent an hour there, thinking about the place and wondering what to do. In the end, as I was just on the point of leaving the small room and heading back the way I had come, I heard some scuffling noises on the other side of the iron door. I pounded again and called out to whomever might be there but got no response. Then the great locking mechanism of the door began to move, as though I were inside an enormous clock just as it prepared to strike the hour. The movement came to a stop with a loud thunk that reverberated around the room. There was a brief pause then and the door opened. It was slow at first, but then I took hold of the handle and pulled it more quickly. I expected some kind of light, but through the door I saw only darkness. Very slowly, and framed by that darkness, I saw the figure of a man emerge. It was only his face at first, but then his upper body came into view. I realized I was standing between the man and the bulb on the door, blocking the light, and I moved to see more clearly. As I did so, the man took a step forward. He was about my age and like me he had dressed for warmer weather. He looked at me as though I might say something, but I didn't know what to say. The man took another small step toward me and looked at me with a petitioning expression. It was clear that he wanted to come through the door, but also that he wanted my permission. I stepped as far to the side as I could and gestured for him to come in. We stood there together for a few moments, both of us waiting for the other to say something. I felt increasingly worried that the door was going to close again and that I might be stuck in this room for even longer. Finally, I excused myself and passed through the open doorway. Turning back, I could no longer see the man there, perhaps because he was now blocking the light. Because it seemed the appropriate thing to do, I pulled the iron door closed behind me. I heard the loud echo of the door latching shut. I examined the door briefly but found no latch or handle that might be used to open it. I wondered how the other man had managed to open the door just now, because I certainly had not been the one to do so.

Outside the seventh door, I found myself in an alley. Initially, because of the high brick walls in front of me and to my left, I thought I was in another prison-like courtyard. Turning right, I saw that the alley opened onto the street. I walked to the end of the alley and onto the sidewalk where the light was low but clear. I looked up and down the length of the street and couldn't see any cars or any other people. I stood there for several long moments, watching for signs of life but finding none. I played with the notion that the city had been evacuated, leaving me alone in it. I began walking down the sidewalk to my right, with no clear agenda and really no sense for which direction might be the best one. Then I recognized a desire, something close to instinct or habit, that pulled me down the street. The building I had just come through was now on my right, and it filled most of this city block. From where I stood, it was nothing more than a long brick wall with very small windows placed high and far out of reach at regular intervals. I decided to keep walking, if slowly, moving toward the corner ahead of me, where I could see, for the first time, people passing by on foot or on bicycle. An occasional car rolled through the intersection. The corner seemed a long way off and I found that fact strangely pleasant and discomfiting at once. I stopped then, looking first at the corner far ahead of me and then back toward the alley, which seemed about the same distance from where I stood. I faced the long, flat side of the building, and didn't move for a long while. For the longest time, I stood there trying to remember where it was I had been going and what I had hoped to accomplish there.

The Two Mr. Greens

The second Mr. Green asks the first Mr. Green what he thinks about this fence of theirs. It's old and rotting, and he wonders if they might do something about it. The first Mr. Green says he's happy to help repair the fence or build a new one. As long as we're just standing here, he says, we might as well get some work done. The second Mr. Green says he'll call the city first thing in the morning. He wants to be sure they won't be digging into buried power lines. In his years, he says, he's found that that one phone call can save a lot of trouble down the line.

The second Mr. Green calls the city and finds that while it's safe to dig, they just need to double check and make sure that the new building will be constructed within his taxable property lines, including any setbacks. An overly polite city employee tells him this should be no problem. It shouldn't take more than a few minutes to locate the original subdivision maps and for the second Mr. Green to verify that his new construction meets any applicable code and doesn't exceed city standards.

The second Mr. Green finds this talk of new construction a little unnecessary. It's a fence, he says, and a replacement fence at that. The two Mr. Greens agree that the bureaucracy is ridiculous, but the first Mr. Green says that this is what home ownership is like around here. Welcome to it, he says.

The first Mr. Green gets a letter in the mail that ought to have been delivered to the second Mr. Green. This is the first time the post office mistakes one Green for the other, but it's likely, the first Mr. Green says, that it won't be the last. He hands the letter over the fence to his neighbor saying, as though it's his fault, that he's sorry for the mistake.

The letter, when the second Mr. Green finally gets around to opening it, says that the city has discovered a problem. It says the property line that divides the lots owned by Mr. Green and Mr. Green is not accurately reflected by the fence. It says that the property line is, in fact, several feet removed from the fence line and the new construction in question must reflect the actual property line and not the current fence line. The new fence, the second Mr. Green is informed, must be built closer to his neighbor's house. This will expand the practical square footage of the second Mr. Green's backyard and will decrease the practical square footage of the first Mr. Green's backyard.

Months pass during which the second Mr. Green memorizes the phone numbers of half a dozen city employees. He fights to gain an exception to the restrictions on new construction that interfere with or disagree with recorded subdivision maps and property boundaries. He gets every city employee he speaks with to admit how wrong it is, how bewildering, that he, a property owner, should not be able to tear down one fence and replace it with another, newer fence without moving the fence several feet and thereby changing the livable space that he and his neighbor have come to know. He gets them to admit that it's beyond reason that he should not be able to build a fence *within* his property line. He gets them to admit that he's actually offering to give up real estate to his neighbor by keeping the fence where it's been, apparently, for decades. They agree and agree but they each say the same thing in the end. They say, I'm sorry Mr. Green, but my hands are tied.

The two Mr. Greens and their wives sit down to dinner at the first Green's house. They decide right then that they will not let the city come between their friendship, that they will follow the city's rules, that they will build the fence as required, and that they won't think about it again. All are agreed, they smile and laugh and raise a glass to friendship. The first Mrs. Green says, Let bygones be bygones, and the night ends as pleasantly as it began.

The two Mr. Greens set to work on the fence. The first Mr. Green refuses to make the second Mr. Green do all the work. He's in this project all the way. They hit the lumberyard, pick out hardware, ask their wives to help decide which wood, which height, which design. They discuss the relative merits of setting cedar posts in packed soil or pressure-treated fir in concrete. They make their decisions and buy the supplies.

The old fence comes out easily. The two Mr. Greens make a pile of old posts and slats and rusted nails in the second Mr. Green's driveway. They backfill the holes where posts had once been. They stand together, where they've become accustomed to standing, but with no fence between them now. They stand on either side of a long strip of exposed soil running across their two yards. The grass from one yard and the grass from the other become one huge lawn with a brown line running down its middle. The second Mr. Green is about to say something to the first Mr. Green before the first Mr. Green stops him short. The first Mr. Green says he knows exactly what the second Mr. Green is thinking and that he appreciates the idea. But no, he says, two yards are two yards and fences are fences.

They measure out the new fence line. They chalk it and mark their post holes, taking turns digging and removing dirt. The second Mr. Green is about to dig a final hole when the first Mr. Green says he'll get the cement started. While the first Mr. Green is gone, the second Mr. Green hits something in the ground not six inches beneath the surface. It's a rock, he assumes at first, like so many he's hit so far. He works to dislodge it or break it. He digs around it, getting deep enough to approach the rock from another angle. What he finds, in the end, is no rock at all. Instead, it's a box.

It's a relatively small metal box, maybe six inches by ten by two. It might have been locked shut at one point, but now the latches are so rusted that they simply break apart in the second Mr. Green's hands. He doesn't pause to consider what might be in the box, doesn't stop to wonder what a person might put in such a thing or why it would be buried here in the first place. Had he paused, he might have considered the possibility of a dead pet or a time capsule. It will make sense to the second Mr. Green later that the box should have contained something mundane, but he doesn't stop to think about it. He simply pries the box open and finds what he finds: plastic bags covering more plastic bags covering a book.

He doesn't shout out that he's found something that the first Mr. Green needs to see. Instead, he does something he'll regret, off and on, in the months to come. He carries the box and book around the side of his house, away from the first Mr. Green. He sneaks, unseen, into his own garage and deposits the box on a shelf there. He'll come back to investigate later. In the meantime, he pops out of the garage, comes up to the first Mr. Green and says, too loudly, that he's got plenty of soda, does his neighbor want a soda?

The ground is marked for digging, the lumber laid out, the cement ready to mix. It's just a matter of throwing things together. The two Mr. Greens find a rhythm and before dusk they're able to stand back and admire their project. They both stand on the same side of the fence, on the second Mr. Green's side of the fence. The first Mr. Green slaps a hand onto the second Mr. Green's shoulder and says they have reason to be proud, that that's one good-looking fence.

It isn't until later, after a backyard barbecue with a cool evening breeze, until after the night has wound down, until after both families have returned to their respective homes, that the second Mr. Green, lying there in bed, remembers the box in his garage. The curiosity eats at him, making sleep impossible. He slips out of bed, careful not to disturb his wife. He sneaks through his own house, into his own garage, past his own car. The concrete is cold beneath his feet and he can feel the oily grit of antifreeze mixed with cat litter. He finds the box and is surprised by the heft of it. He doesn't remember this weight. He doesn't remember this rust. He opens the box with some small effort, removes the bags from the box and then the book from the bags. The book itself is thicker than its own spine, the pages swollen with moisture. The spine cracks and pops when he forces it back on itself. The first pages he sees are blank except for faint blue lines, a faint red margin: a diary of empty pages. But there at the front he finds that some of the pages are covered neatly in a steady, even hand. This is, the second Mr. Green sees, a diary with only one entry. Twelve pages.

He wants to know who wrote it. He wants to know an author's name before he reads, but there's nothing that tells. There's no evidence that the author of this entry meant for him to read it. He reads anyway. He reads a confession that seems less than remarkable, the account of a young woman who, at the age of seventeen, got comfortable with a boyfriend. A baby follows, but the young mother has no chance to be a young mother. They send the baby to another home. They send the young girl to live with an aunt, far from her shame. They are her parents, the aunt is an aunt, but these roles get reversed, and before long she feels for the aunt what she never felt for her parents. The aunt understands, appreciates, empathizes. The parents disappear for long stretches, making few attempts at contact. She feels abandoned for a mistake she made, but worse, feels that she is, to them, only the mistake she made. She has been reduced to one bad decision, to one behavior that, while not something she's proud of, was natural, was exactly what anyone would have wanted in her situation. They told her the baby went to a good home. She believes them because she has no reason not to, but she fears for the welfare of that child. She's older now, this unnamed confessor. She has a husband. She never means to tell him this one fact about her past, but she's writing it down because she feels she must.

The second Mr. Green wonders what the first Mr. Green knows and what he doesn't know. He assumes the book belonged to someone living in that other house and wonders if it belonged to the Green family or to some previous owner. The book seems old enough that it might have spent decades buried in the yard. He considers Mrs. Green, his neighbor, and wonders if the book is hers. If it is, wouldn't she remember that she buried it? Wouldn't she remember the spot? Wouldn't she have seen where they were digging and done something to stop them, to intervene and rescue the book from discovery? Then, of course, he wonders if maybe she buried it for exactly this purpose, hoping that someday it would be discovered, dug up, brought to light. Then he remembers something else. He remembers that the Greens next door have older children and while he assumed that their married daughter, the one living just a few miles away, was in fact their biological child, maybe she's a niece, so fully embraced and made to feel at home, so fully estranged from her own parents that she's adopted the Greens as her only family.

The second Mr. Green finds himself at an impasse. He would like to think, having read this unburied confession, that he knows something, but what does he know other than the relatively spare details of a story he hears all the time? Okay, maybe not all the time, but often enough. What of it? He needs to wrap the book back in its plastic bags and back in the box and take it to the Greens. He can say he found it while digging. He can say he meant to hand it over sooner but got distracted. He can pretend that he never opened it, pretend that he did the right thing and handed property over to the people whose yard it was buried in, even if that yard is not theirs anymore. But then won't he be giving the first Mr. Green no choice but to read what he has read? This won't work. The second Mr. Green anticipates what might happen. He imagines the conversations in which he feigns ignorance of the book and how he might, accidentally, say too much. He has to consider the woman who wrote this thing. Maybe she buried it for the obvious reason that she didn't want it found, and his discovery, accidental as it was, was only a near miss, a discovery by one who could be unaffected by the information found there. The secret's safe with him. Shouldn't that be the right thing to do? Shouldn't he maintain the confidence of this woman he knows only through her buried book? He decides to keep his mouth shut, but wonders what to do with the book itself. If he wraps it up and throws it away, won't he then have interfered? Didn't someone take the time to write this thing, to dig a hole in the earth, and bury it?

He realizes that he wants desperately to know what his neighbor, the first Mr. Green, really knows. They stand there, these two neighbors, and they talk about the innocuous things they talk about, and all the time the second Mr. Green wonders whether the first Mr. Green knows his wife has a secret. He wonders if the first Mr. Green knows that somewhere in his wife's past there's this indiscretion. He wonders what happens when the first Mr. Green and the first Mrs. Green talk about their respective families and their early years, before they met and married. The second Mr. Green is long gone, oblivious to the conversation he's ostensibly having with the first Mr. Green, lost instead in the series of questions that have now come into his head. The first Mr. Green smiles and laughs and says he can't believe a person would do such a thing. The second Mr. Green has no idea what the first Mr. Green is talking about, but he takes his cue, laughs along, says he knows exactly what his neighbor means.

There's only one option, the second Mr. Green decides. He must rebury the box, put it back where he found it and pretend that he never found it in the first place. Piece of cake, he decides. There are some logistical problems, of course. He knows that to bury the box where it was is impossible, because that space is now filled with cement and a fence post. So, he'll have to get as close as possible.

He waits until midnight, heads outside with a headlamp, and sets to work. He digs a hole very near the fence post and its cement foundation. The ground is moist and turns easily. The rocks he expected to find are not there. The hard clay is not there. He's shocked at the ease with which his spade reaches deeper and deeper into the earth. He gets as deep as the base of the cement, a full three feet beneath the sod and then goes a few inches deeper. He decides that this fence won't last forever and this secret shouldn't either. He sets the box at the base of the cement where it will surely be discovered in ten or twenty years when this fence comes out to be replaced by a newer one. That's a solution he feels absolutely at peace with. Now he has managed to delay the discovery of this secret, which is better than immediate revelation or destruction. He's found a way to remove himself from the equation.

The earth he dug is quickly returned to itself and the sod he had to cut away is replaced neatly, expertly. Clean-up is a snap. But as he's standing there, admiring his own work, something catches his eye. This is trouble. A light has gone off inside the first Mr. Green's house and it might have been anything. It's two in the morning and that light might have been on for hours or it might have been on for an instant, but it's certainly off now. He should have paid closer attention and he regrets what he didn't take note of in advance. It might have been a bathroom down a hallway where someone made a middle of the night visit. It might have been a refrigerator catching someone satisfying a craving. It might have been a flashlight. It might have been an observer, peeking out to see just what this neighbor was up to. The specifics don't matter. What matters is that lights do not simply go out in the middle of the night. Someone must have been up. Someone must have been awake in that mostly darkened house where they would so easily have been alarmed by the sight of the second Mr. Green's head-mounted flashlight bobbing up and down in the night. The second Mr. Green saw enough to know that something or other flashed inside that house, it flickered. There was light there for a moment. He might have some explaining to do.

While the second Mr. Green would like to avoid the first Mr. Green—would like, in fact, to simply stay away from that fence for a day or two—he knows that he really should be as neighborly as possible in the hope that nothing was seen, and nothing has changed. Returning from work, he goes outside and sees the first Mr. Green raking leaves on the far side of his yard. The first Mr. Green is nearly done with his work, and the second Mr. Green expects that once his neighbor has finished stuffing that last bag he'll come to the fence to chat. He doesn't come, though. He just nods his head, a distant hello, and disappears into his house.

The second Mr. Green is puzzled by the behavior of the first Mr. Green. He thinks about what he did that night and what his neighbor might have thought if, in fact, one of them looked out and saw him digging. He knows that the first Mr. Green is likely to be curious and is just as likely to question him about his late-night yard work. That the first Mr. Green hasn't asked such questions bothers the second Mr. Green who begins to feel a little angry at his neighbor. After all, he was digging on his side of the fence, and he had every right to. This neighbor of his could think what he wanted, but the second Mr. Green was doing nothing wrong. Or rather, if the second Mr. Green was doing something wrong, the first Mr. Green couldn't have known it, could only know that his neighbor was doing something strange and worthy of a few pointed questions. The real problem, the second Mr. Green finally admits to himself, is that he has prepared an airtight explanation for his behavior and wishes his neighbor would ask what he was doing, digging so late at night, so that he can rehearse the invented details of his explanation. He's tired of carrying this revised history around with him and wishes the first Mr. Green would admit already that he saw the second Mr. Green digging in the night so he can shed this fiction of his.

It's days before the first Mr. Green comes to the fence again. When he does, he comes with apologies. He hasn't been sleeping well, he says, and he's sorry to have been so unneighborly, but the sleepless nights are killing him. The first Mr. Green asks the second Mr. Green what he knows about insomnia. The second Mr. Green says that he doesn't know a whole lot. Then the first Mr. Green says that he figured as much. He says that he took his neighbor for the kind of man who sleeps like a baby, right through the night. The second Mr. Green doesn't know whether he's just been let off the hook or caught in the act. He doesn't know if his neighbor has just identified the extinguished light in his house that night as an inconsequential flicker caused by a sleepless man, or whether he's just said, as plainly as he could, that he's been watching the second Mr. Green and knows something is up. The second Mr. Green is about to say something about burying a child's pet hamster when he realizes what a non sequitur it would be. He says nothing and smiles like a man he is, one helpless to understand insomnia.

The second Mr. Green decides to be a detective. He needs to know what his neighbors know about him and about each other. He decides that he can learn the identity of his unknown confessor by simply asking the right questions. He's new in the neighborhood, after all, and don't people expect him to ask for some basic questions about background and history and origins? Would it be so strange for one neighbor to ask another neighbor where he or she was born, where he or she was raised? He doesn't have to come out and ask the first Mr. Green if he knows his wife had another man's child before she had one with him. He doesn't have to ask the first Mrs. Green whether she or her daughter has a secret to keep. He doesn't have to ask if that daughter is really a niece. It's much easier than that. He'll simply reveal a thing or two about himself and wait for everyone else to do the same.

The second Mr. Green talks to his wife, proposes having the Greens over for dinner. She thinks it's a fine idea, so he invites the neighbors and they accept. So far so good. They sit down over roasted vegetables, pork loin, green salad. They make pleasant conversation about the virtues of eating from one's own garden. They talk about the simultaneous joy and worry and stress of parenting. They talk about the upcoming holiday (Halloween). The second Mr. Green feels that he must step in and ask a question or two, say something that will move the conversation in a better direction. As his wife says something about alternatives to handing out candy, he says that he doesn't know a thing about where his neighbors grew up. That was wrong, wasn't it? He meant to speak first and let the Greens follow his lead, but now he's come right out and asked them what he hoped to tease out slowly. The first Mr. Green seems unalarmed and indifferent. He says that both he and his wife are from here. That's the word he uses: here. As though they were both raised in the same exact place. The second Mr. Green makes a joke about the Greens growing up in his house. The others laugh at this politely, but the second Mr. Green laughs too hard. This is going nowhere. The first Mrs. Green says that she and her husband met in high school, teenage sweethearts and all that. She looks the second Mr. Green directly in the eye when she speaks. She might be staring him down. She might be warning him to drop his questions right this instant. It's at this moment that he remembers what the first Mrs. Green said, weeks earlier, about letting bygones be bygones. Was it a clue? he wonders. Did she reveal, in the use of an idiom, that it was her book he'd found? He feels the first Mrs. Green watching him, staring at him. He refuses to meet her eye. He refuses to know, for sure, whether she's even looking his way.

He learned nothing in his attempt to catch a confession from the Greens. Almost nothing. He knows that they went to high school together. This means, he decides, that if the first Mrs. Green wrote the confession he found in the space beneath his new fence, then she would have had a baby, adopted it away, and then almost immediately crossed paths with her future husband. This is impossible, the second Mr. Green decides. He can think of nothing else but the hypothetical history of his neighbors. They're such nice people. Why would he want to know their indiscretions? He decides he can save himself a lot of grief by letting the whole thing go.

Later, the second Mrs. Green asks her husband if he knew that the first Mr. Green had sleeping problems. The second Mr. Green says that the first Mr. Green was just telling him about it the other day. The second Mrs. Green says that the first Mrs. Green says that it's been like this for years but that the problem comes and goes. She says that the medications are apparently some help but that the first Mr. Green is reluctant to take them. The first Mrs. Green also says that her husband won't admit it, but that his inability to sleep is directly linked to stress. It's his work, she says. He brings all that worry home with him and keeps it company through the night.

The second Mr. Green begins to feel that his neighbors are multiplying. He knows the Mr. and Mrs. Green who live next door. He knows their children. He also knows the Mrs. Green who buried a confession and the one who didn't, the one who had a child out of wedlock and the one who didn't. He knows the Mr. Green who knows that his wife has another child and the Mr. Green who doesn't know. He knows the Greens who raised a niece like a daughter after she made a mistake, and the Greens who raised a daughter like a daughter and have her over for dinner most Sundays. He knows the Mr. Green who helped him build a fence, the Mr. Green whose job is taxing, the Mr. Green who saw his neighbor's unusual behavior in the night. He knows the Greens from whom he has taken property and ought to begrudge him. He knows the Greens who are neighborly and have no capacity for spite. He knows the Greens who know what he knows and the Greens who don't, the Greens who are grateful to have seen him rebury what never belonged to him, the Greens who don't know that what they buried was ever uncovered, the Greens who buried nothing, the Greens who resent him, the Greens who admire him, the Greens who are oblivious, the Greens who peer into his windows at night, the Greens who have forgotten their own regrets, the Greens with nothing to forget, the Greens who can't sleep.

The Scold

S*he's just standing there* in the doorway. We have to wonder why she's standing there, like someone who sees a doorway not as a thing to pass through, but as a thing to stand in, making a point by not passing through, refusing to pass through. Why is she standing there in our doorway—it is ours—and not passing through and not going away and not saying more than she's saying? What does she want? She must want something. Standing in the doorway like that must mean something.

She has asked us to be considerate of others who might be nearby, who might live on the other sides of these walls so thin they hardly support a nail, these walls so thin they hardly contain the heat we all pay too much for.

Are we inconsiderate people? Are ours the actions of people who fail to consider others? This look that passes between us, this look that hangs in the air like our frozen breath, this look says that we don't think we're the people she thinks we are. This looks says that one of us should say to the woman that we're not culprits if culprits are what she's after. This look is content to assume the passive voice and say that perhaps a mistake has been made.

The baby, she says, the baby. And we say, The baby? And she says it would take so little. A little consideration is all it would take. All she asks, she says, standing there in the doorway that is very clearly ours and not hers is that perhaps we might consider others a bit more than we have. Here she raises up just a little, pushes forward onto the balls of her feet, stretches her neck like she's a bird. She leans through the doorway that is ours and not hers, peers into the space that is ours and not hers, looking for the baby: that sweet, sweet, inconsiderate baby.

We're not inconsiderate people. We're not, of course, unaware of these thin walls that do so little to muffle sounds not meant for other ears. Haven't we wished for walls just a bit thicker than these? But the baby? The baby is a baby. The baby has been a perfect baby, an ideal baby, a model baby. The baby has performed baby-ness with such perfection, such total perfection.

We haven't slept well, it's true. We've smiled our thin smiles and said to each other that one day, soon enough, we might refer back to this exhaustion as others have done (have claimed to have done). There have already been moments we regret, moments in which we have said oh, hell, or dammit, or when we sighed so heavily it was as though we had cursed the graves of our grandmothers. There have been these moments—these moments that are ours, that belong to us and us alone—that are no business of this woman whose head, like a periscope, keeps searching for the inconsiderate baby.

We haven't told her she can't come through the doorway. We haven't told her she can. We opened the door, as considerate people would. We said hello and smiled, as considerate people do. We allowed our brows to wrinkle, our faces to assume expressions of consternation, as any considerate people would, when she said that there was something the matter, something in need of correction. Our heads bobbed up and down in a continuous state of agreement. Our heads said everything there was to say: that we're considerate people who will listen to the pleas of a hunched, old woman, who will wait patiently through her senseless preamble, who will speak in hushed tones when hushed tones are appropriate.

But the baby? The perfect baby? The sweet baby that is ours and not hers? There has been crying, certainly. Oh, how our sweet, perfect baby cries when crying is necessary, when crying is the perfect, sweet, appropriate thing for a baby to do. Oh, how our baby cries when a baby ought to cry, when a baby must cry, when a baby would be mistaken not to cry. All that crying, oh sweet baby, the crying you can do. It's part of the equation, isn't it? Isn't there an equation somewhere that always ends with crying, that must end with crying? Isn't crying at the end of that equation and others, too? Weren't we told to brace ourselves for this? Weren't we?

She cranes her neck, clearly dissatisfied. She allows her weight, the little there is of it, to fall back to where it belongs, on her side of the doorway, the side that is not ours, the side that is also not exactly hers. Her face has this thing about it, this fixity. Her face is so perfectly unchanging. Her eyes are wide open but seem so flat and sleepy. Her lips are thin and form a perfectly straight line that looks as though it has never smiled. Her face is perfect and awful. Her face is mean. Her face is ready, at any moment, to assume a scowl, to glower.

May I? she says, using her hands to suggest she's giving us something. She turns her palms toward us and opens her arms as though to escort herself into the room. No, we say, you may not. That does the trick. That puts a little curve in her perfectly straight, perfectly flat, perfectly vile little mouth. Then we apologize, make our own gestures—palms to the chest as though clutching our own hearts—and say, the baby, the poor, sweet thing. The baby, we say, and we shake our heads and purse our lips and let our hands come together like an empty cup before us to show exactly how sorry we are. The baby, we say. Finally getting some sleep, we say. Thank the heavens, we say.

The baby, she says, we must consider the baby. The horizon of her mouth has found its equilibrium. Absolutely, we say. We can hardly tell you how happy we are that the baby is finally getting some sleep. Yes, she says, we must consider the baby.

She's on the other side of the door, the side that is not ours. She's in the hallway. She's in the hallway that is not ours and not hers. She has every right to stand there in the hallway. She has every right. We thank her for nothing in particular. We whisper good night as though we just remembered to keep our voices very low, as though we have developed a sudden, pressing need for stealth. We give the door a nudge, a quiet little nudge, and let it close gently, quietly, as though of its own accord.

Blight

M*elville knows exactly* what his wife's body looks like. He's seen it so many times and for so many years, that he thinks he must know it better than she does. If her body has changed, he knows exactly how it's done so. He's watched her arms and legs as they've dropped a certain, obvious strength only to be replaced by so much drooping skin, a loose covering for bones. The changes are virtually imperceptible, but he knows that every time he sees her she will be slightly shorter and slightly lighter. He can't help himself from startling when she enters the room. To see her coming through a doorway as though at some great distance is like a play of forced perspective. He sees her and he knows that something terrible has happened and that they've only managed to convince themselves otherwise. In these moments, Melville feels the need to race to the phone and call for an ambulance. He needs to shelter his wife, protect her from the forces wearing down her health and vitality. He wants to scream to the neighbors that something is wrong. He catches himself with these thoughts only after his wife has caught him staring. At first, she asked what he was thinking. At first, she acted as though she wasn't becoming a ghost. But now, after so much silence, he finds her staring back in disgust. Her eyes betray revulsion. He doesn't know if her condition is accelerating. He doesn't know if there are hopeful signs that his shrinking wife is shrinking less rapidly than she once did. He wonders if in the absence of medical advice and observation they have missed clear indicators that the end is near. He doesn't know what it is anymore when he thinks about the end. Is the end of her illness the beginning of recovery or is it the beginning of his life without her? He's spent too much time thinking about what comes next, after he's been forced to admit that he really should have insisted on seeing one more doctor, and then one more, and then one more. He doesn't want to acknowledge that his thoughts are filled with a kind of empty happiness, filled with a sense of sadness and relief, as if he were longing for the day when his loss might finally take precedence over hers. Does he want his wife to shrink and shrink and finally disappear? Does he feel guilty for believing that there's only one end to this suffering? Melville looks at his wife, propped on a pile of blankets, as she watches Peter Lorre in some old black-and-white movie. He watches her and thinks about life without her and regrets his inability to imagine improvement. Melville looks at his wife and wonders how long it will be before she's half the size she used to be. He wonders when she'll cross that threshold.

The doctors said her blood work looked good and that her vitals were where they ought to be. They said she was the picture of health and ought to keep up her good habits. When they asked if there were concerns or questions, she said there weren't. When they said, Great, and began to stand, reaching to shake her hand or open the door, she asked if they were sure nothing at all was wrong. What did she mean? they wanted to know. Everything looked good. There were no worrying signs. She was just worried, she said, about those things she couldn't control. She thought about a cancer that might be growing inside of her. She thought about osteoporosis. She thought about dementia and renal failure and a slowly weakening heart. She admitted that these fears were unfounded, and she knew she was foolish to embrace them as she did, but wasn't it reasonable for her to be unreasonable now and again? She was a worrier, she said, and was inclined to this mild hypochondria. The doctors laughed at that and said it was perfectly normal to be concerned for one's health, but that there was really nothing at all to worry about. What she didn't tell any of the doctors was that she weighed a good deal less than she used to and that she had once been several inches taller than she was then. If she was the picture of health, she said to Melville, it was a smaller picture than it used to be. In time, she stopped seeing doctors altogether. They said the same things, of course, but because she refused to see the same doctor twice, Melville felt uncertain about her motivations. She had seen maybe a dozen by the end, but the end of those appointments was only the beginning of her new life indoors. She became what she called her husband's kept wife. She laughed at that and asked where in the world his sense of humor had gone. Melville knew there was nothing funny about this small woman lying in bed next to him. This was a tragedy, he said, or a medical mystery, but it wasn't funny.

When his phone rings, Melville answers, then listens, then says he'll check and puts his thumb over the microphone. His wife, sitting across the table on a booster seat he made from two-by-eights, tilts her head and waits for him to say who it is. It's a neighbor named Carol who refuses to stop calling. Each time her excuse is just as flimsy. Is your wife at home, she wants to know, because she's making this pie crust, and his wife knows all the secrets. Melville's wife has never made a pie crust, much less a pie, and he wonders why this Carol woman doesn't just call his wife directly. Of course he knows she wouldn't answer. Carol must know this, too. He mouths Carol's name to his wife who then rolls her eyes. Melville says he'll just go grab his wife and holds the receiver to his ear. He slouches as though it's a real burden just pretending to look. He listens to Carol breathing deeply into her phone. He wonders what she's thinking and wonders if she knows he's lying. He wonders how many more times she'll call before she starts knocking on the door or peeking through windows. His wife moves her hand to suggest that he get on with it already. He uncovers the microphone, clears his throat, and says that he was sure his wife was home, but apparently she isn't. He'll have her call, he says. She must know, Melville thinks, that she's being avoided. It's strange, Melville says to Carol, she was just here.

Having driven ten hours to the coast, having escaped the cold air and gray skies, and the various signs of winter illness all around them, Melville and his wife stretched out under an enormous awning and watched the waves of the Pacific Ocean rolling and rolling. Melville's wife dug her feet through the sand and said there was nothing she enjoyed so much as this. She pushed her feet in deeper and then pulled them out by leaning back and bringing her knees up nearly to her chin. The sand poured between her toes and left her feet dusty with those fine, sparkling particles. She said there was nothing she loved like wiggling her toes through sand and feeling the heat on her body and listening to the waves breaking into and over each other. Melville looked at his wife and watched as she buried her feet in the sand again, and as she removed them again. He looked at those small pyramids on the top sides of her bare feet. He saw the sand sliding away in little rivers.

She weighs about a third of what she did on their wedding day, stands quite a bit shorter. None of her old clothes fit except for a couple of sweatshirts she wears like enormous blankets. Melville watches his wife lying there in bed, listens to her make plans for the day, and wonders how she can be so calm about all this. She says she needs him to get an oil change before the week is over and that she can't remember but she's pretty sure they're out of milk. Melville says the milk won't be a problem, but he's not sure when he can get the car in. Oh, he almost forgot, his sister called to say something about a friend of hers, an orthopedic surgeon. His wife stares at him as though there must be more to what he's saying. She asks what he told his sister. He told her nothing. She's the one who brought it up, saying something about friends they had over for dinner. He said nothing at all about his wife. She never entered the conversation. I was just thinking, he says. I've told you, she says, that I'm through with doctors. The worst part is how hard they work to make it seem like they're not stumped, as though they really might have answers. Melville wants to know why his wife is so stubborn about all this, why she won't just give this new doctor fifteen minutes, maybe an x-ray or two. Right, she says, just like every other time. Melville watches his wife pull the covers up to her face and turn toward the wall. He hears nothing.

She wanted to stay up late, she said. She wanted to watch the stars even though it was cold out and the clouds had been heavy all afternoon. It was okay, she said. She wanted to bundle up and lie back on the lawn to see what they could see. Melville carried dozens of blankets outside and made a bed of them. They squeezed together under that heavy pile. They watched their breath turn white in the air above them and then drift off into nothing. They saw the lights from the city reflecting against the clouds and waited for holes in the canopy. That one is Sirius, Melville said, the Dog Star. Is it really? she said. Might be, he said. What's that? she said, pointing to another break in the clouds. That, he said, is Orion's foot. And that? That's the tail of either Pegasus or Ursa Minor. And that's the last star in the big dipper's handle, and that's one of Jupiter's moons and that's part of the Southern Cross that wanders north this time of year, and that's just a Soviet satellite that somebody forgot to shoot down. You're good at this, she said. Yeah, he said, pretty good.

Melville's wife says she isn't sure what the point is. Those are just empty calories, she says. Melville, holding an energy bar, says that it will serve to help with the exhaustion. Melville's wife wants to know what exhaustion he means. She wants to know what in the world he's talking about. Melville knows what he's talking about because it's written all over his wife's shrinking body. She's weaker than she's ever been. She can hardly move without becoming short of breath. Still, he struggles to remember if his wife has ever claimed exhaustion or if it's just something he's observed. Well, he says, and then he pauses because nothing comes to mind. Then he lies and says that he remembers her saying something about feeling a little lethargic. She doesn't have a clue what he's talking about, she says. In fact, she doesn't remember when she ever felt this alive. Energy, she says, is something she doesn't lack. What he's talking about is probably something he made up. What he's talking about is gibberish. Later, when he sets a slice of cheesecake in front of her, she pushes it away and says, No, thank you. It's been the same every time, with her saying that he should eat her portion, or that he should enjoy that piece of pie, or that cake, or that sweet roll all by himself. He deserves it, she says, he has the right to indulge. This sliver of a woman isn't the person he married. In many ways, he feels that his wife is a stranger who has crept into his life.

Melville remembers standing there, on the back patio, listening to his wife explain that he never listened, not really. She said that maybe, just once, he might take her opinions into account. He meant to. He knew that she needed to say these things and that he needed to focus for a couple of minutes, and that if he did maybe things would improve. He looked at his wife, near her, but also at the sunlight coming from behind her, and all he could think was that the light was coming from the wrong place. He knew that just the day before at this same time the sun was shining through that row of cottonwoods behind her to the right. So, if the time was the same and it was only the next day, but the sun had moved so far along the horizon, something must have changed. Every variable he could think to consider: the time, the place, his position, suggested that something was wrong, and he could only assume it was him, because last he checked the heavens had a pretty good track record. She said that he wasn't doing a very good job, even then. She could tell, she said, that he wasn't paying attention to her at that very moment, that his thoughts were elsewhere. Then suddenly she was talking about the history of the universe and how that sun of theirs was going to burn out before too long, but that those billions of years between now and then were clearly so much more than they needed, that they had plenty of time, time in excess. The life they could have had was still the life they might have. Melville tried to keep his thoughts on his wife, tried to consider what she said, but all he could think was how weird it was that he was thinking about the sun and she was talking about the sun but that what she said and what he thought were not causally linked, that the relationship between her utterance and his thought was one of simultaneity but not interdependence. Listen, she said then, would you just listen? She had nothing more to say, nothing for him to listen to. She exhaled heavily and stared over his shoulder as if he wasn't there.

His wife has lost another ten pounds. She smiles weakly when she tells him. It's as though she were saying it's his fault, or maybe she's proud of herself because she saw it coming. As he stands here behind her, watching her twirl and spin and adjust, he sees that this skirt—the one he bought for her in the children's section of a department store—is his best effort yet. It's simple enough and black and as elegant as children's clothing can be. She seems happy for the surprise of it all, but as he stands here, watching the reflection of her face more than he watches the skirt, he sees that she's less happy now than she was five minutes ago. She loves the skirt but seems dissatisfied with how it fits her. She pulls her face into a puzzled scowl and watches herself in their full-length mirror, sure that something is wrong but unsure just what. When he asks what the trouble is, she says she doesn't know. It fits perfectly, she says, but it doesn't look like it fits perfectly. Look, she says, and she pulls her shirt up just above her waist to show him just how perfect the fit is, but then she turns back to the mirror, waves her hand to indicate everything she can see there. It's too short, she says, or maybe it's too long. All she knows is that it hits her knees wrong and seems to cut her legs in half. She says it makes her feel even shorter than she is. No, he says, it's perfect. No, she says, just look at it.

At that dinner party, still months before she decided to keep herself indoors, no one could get over how good Melville's wife looked. They said it again and again. Melville stared at his shoes while the host made a big show of not knowing what his wife had done to herself, saying that she just couldn't believe how good they both looked. But the host wasn't talking about him. She held his wife by the shoulders, looked her up and down, amazed, she said, just amazed by that stunning dress. I wish I had your style, the host said. Melville wanted to shout at that. He wanted to tell this woman to quit the act already because it wasn't doing anyone any good. Instead, he rubbed his chin and wondered when he had last shaved. He wondered if anyone had noticed that his pants were fraying at the cuff and that a hole was starting to form below the left knee. The host continued, saying that she simply had to know the secret. It was suffocating, that environment, and he wanted to be free of it. He could see how the accentuated disbelief confused his wife who made a play at gratitude and did such a fine job looking both pleased and embarrassed at once. She accepted the compliments the only way she knew how, with just a hint of pride as she deflected attention. If that was it, if the conversation and the evening had ended there, everything might have been fine for a while longer. But he knew what was going to happen long before it did. He knew that the conversation would return to health and nutrition and the apparent secret his wife was keeping. He knew that every lull and every break would be another excuse for someone to say again how they just couldn't get over it, that she looked fantastic. It was all so pathetic the way they tried to get her to confess something, the way they encouraged her to announce her secret while pretending they weren't prying. None of them wanted to be the one to ask if it was time at the gym, or a change in diet, or maybe something a doctor was giving her. He knew that through it all she would hardly touch her dinner, nibbling only enough to justify a comment about an amazing dish, wondering what herb this was, what spice, or treating the things on her plate as objects to occupy her busy hands. In the end, she rearranged more than she ate, as though she were a child, forced to stay at the table, refusing to finish her greens. Later, he wondered what his wife thought of all that silliness at the party. He asked what she thought of the fuss people made. Yes, she said, wasn't it something? It was crazy, Melville said, the way everyone pretended not to stare. Pretty juvenile, if you ask me, but no one asked Melville anything and he watched his wife watching herself in the floor-length mirror. She spun slowly and made her dress wrap around her legs just a little, following her movements by half a second. Melville saw the little smile on his wife's face and knew that even now she was enjoying all the attention. It really is a nice dress, she said, and she turned to Melville and held his gaze. You did all right, she said. She turned back to the mirror then and he saw the reflection of her face, smiling at something he couldn't see.

The loose skin on her arms and on her legs and at her waist makes it clear that she's a smaller version of the person she used to be. Melville's wife is too young to look so fragile, too young to look so much like an old woman. Each time he sees her, he learns again, as though for the first time, that his wife is shrinking and that he's helpless to do anything about it. She sits now, with her legs crossed, her feet resting on her thighs in a way Melville imagines to be uncomfortable. Her spine is straight. She has excellent posture. She sits on the bedroom floor and moves her upper body in a small but perceptible circle. Her oscillations are a quiet reminder that she's lost in thought or trying to be. If he asks, she will claim to be meditating, breathing deeply so as to be mindful of her body, but he can hear the struggle in her lungs, the rasp that has become more pronounced with time. She isn't well, but she has made it clear that she doesn't want to talk about it. Melville wonders where his wife goes when she disappears this way. He wonders how long it's been since they talked about anything important. He wonders when he last touched her body in a way that wasn't merely accidental, brushing by her in the hallway or leaning into her very slightly while sitting on the couch. He wonders how long it's been since anything passed between them that he might consider a form of intimacy. He leaves the room as quietly as he entered it.

Melville felt the moisture seeping into his socks and knew that he should have worn different shoes. The snow was six inches deep on the lawn and in the street, but only half that on the driveway and sidewalk he'd already shoveled twice in three hours. The snow looked light enough but was really a heavy slush. He knew his back was going to ache. He also knew that he was supposed to find some pleasure in all this. He was supposed to see all the snow as a wonder of nature, as a mystery, as evidence of great symmetry in the natural world. He was supposed to listen to the muffled sounds around him and wonder at the enormity of so much snow. He was supposed to take a handful of new flakes and marvel that they had taken as long as an hour to fall so far from their points of origin. He was supposed to throw that handful into the air and note the way it changed dull light into something marvelous, but he could feel a stinging pain in his cheeks and in his ears and in his toes. There was nothing to enjoy about this. As he continued to shovel snow into tall piles at either side of his driveway, he wondered if the noise of the shovel scrapping on concrete was keeping his wife awake. It probably was. He wondered if she was, at that very moment, covering her head with a pillow and resenting his efforts. He kept shoveling, kept scraping, kept moving his toes against the soupy mush filling his shoes.

Some people shrink, Melville's wife says. What people is she referring to? Melville wants to know. Old people? Is that what you mean? Because old people don't shrink so much as they appear to shrink. Old people bend or stoop. Old people have trouble with their posture. This is different, he says. This is something to freak out about. Look, she says, we don't know what this is. Maybe it's just something we'll look back on and laugh about. Maybe it's not what it seems. Melville wants to open the bathroom door and usher his wife into that small room where he knows she keeps a record of her diminishing height and weight. He wants to show her that he knows about the pencil marks and the tallies that she must think she's been hiding behind the door, beneath the hanging towel neither of them ever uses. He wants her to look at the steady decline marked out on the wall and acknowledge that this is not something that simply happens. This, he wants to say, is not natural. People do not get smaller like this.

Melville's wife coughed and coughed. She had piled up dozens of crumpled tissues on the bedside table, and the humidifier purred away. She wondered if he would be a doll and make her some more tea, please. Her voice was worn down and she swallowed heavily. Sure, he said, anything else? No, she said, unless he had managed to find that cure for the cold as he had promised he would. I'm working on that, he said. His wife was sick again and he wanted to remind her that she never used to get sick at all. He wanted to remind her that it had been one thing or another for months now, and that maybe it was time to see someone. He thought better of joking that she was going to exhaust their savings if she kept up her over-the-counter drug habit. Before he turned to leave, his wife asked if he loved her. What? he said. Do you love me? she said. He wanted to know what she meant, and she said it wasn't a complicated question. She laughed and said that his confusion was perhaps the best answer she was going to get. Melville said no, that of course he loved her. He only wondered what had motivated the question. I'm sorry, he said. I love you. She watched him and said nothing, and he stammered a little when he said again that he did love her. His voice was a pale, weak thing. Look, he said, but she cut him off and said that she'd just been thinking about how good he was to her and how well he cared for her, but through it all she'd begun to wonder if a person could truly love someone he cared for in this way. You do so much for me, she said, but what do I do for you? Melville heard the question and the resentment it seemed to veil. His wife said again that he really did such a good job helping her and making her comfortable. Melville just nodded as he considered the distance between caring about a person and caring for one.

Melville's wife, standing on a chair, preparing a salad for herself while Melville slices cheese for a sandwich, asks Melville if he would look in the pantry to see if there are any canned beets. There are beets and he knows she knows it. There are always beets in the pantry, right there on the middle shelf. There must be twenty cans of the things because she has him buy more every time she sends him for groceries. He doesn't answer her question, though, because it occurs to him almost immediately that she isn't asking whether or not they have any beets, but rather, if he would please get them for her. He's willing to do so, he's always willing, but just as soon as he realizes what she really wants, he sees that he was wrong about that, too. She isn't asking him to save her the effort of getting a can of beets from the pantry. She's asking him to do something she can no longer do for herself. Those beets, always at eye level, always right there when he opens the pantry door, are no longer on a shelf she can see or reach. She has lost her ability to get to that shelf without the help of a stepladder or a husband. In that moment, it becomes clear to him that she isn't going to acknowledge her problem unless he forces the issue. He asks her how she's feeling and makes sure to emphasize the question in a way that distinguishes it from the casual chitchat it might be mistaken for. He wants her to hear the question as a doctor might ask it. He puts down his knife, turns his body fully around so he's facing her and asks how she's feeling. She takes a moment to recognize the gravity of his question. She keeps slowly chopping bell peppers, and then, after a pause, knife hanging in the air above the cutting board, she looks at him sidelong, as if she knows what he's up to and refuses to play along. As if he's a stranger forcing himself on her and she's weighing whether to scream or run for help. Then she turns, though not fully, and stares up at him, still holding her knife, to ask whether he's going to get those beets for her or not. It comes to this: if she isn't going to allow him to acknowledge the obvious, then he isn't going to enable her. She can, he tells her, get the beets herself, she knows where they are. She takes her cutting board, overcrowded now with sliced lettuce, cucumbers, and peppers. She tilts the board up and uses her knife to push everything into the sink. Good night, she says, as she steps down from her chair and leaves him alone in the kitchen.

They had been to the park that day, watching young families trying to feed ducks at the edges of a man-made lake. They saw it every time they went there: mothers with strollers and fathers with cameras, nudging their children ever closer to those aggressive, hungry flocks. They might have said something to those parents, but what business was it of theirs? In so many ways, that day was no different. There was the mother watching over a sleeping newborn. There was the father with his camera poised. There was a girl, no more than five, holding a bag of store-bought bread in one hand and a single slice of that bread in the other. The father pushed his daughter closer to the birds even as she resisted. You'll be fine, he said, you'll be fine. They can't hurt you, he said. The poor girl had already lost her smile by then, afraid and wishing she could be finished with this thing. The ducks were closing in and it was obvious to Melville what was going to happen next. When it did, when the girl began to scream and the ducks became frenzied, Melville watched as that father kept the camera to his eye, determined to a get his picture and perhaps frozen by the gap between what he planned and what he got. Melville saw his own wife running into that chaos, shouting at the birds, moving her arms wildly so as to scare them off by a few feet at least, hoping to give the girl space enough to flee, but when she got there, just feet from that girl, the girl didn't run. Instead, she stopped screaming and stared at Melville's wife with wide-eyed terror, as though this woman was far more frightening than all those too-familiar birds. She stared at Melville's wife and then took two steps back, before turning and running to hide behind her father. For his part, the father looked more embarrassed than anything, sheepish perhaps because he had allowed a stranger to rescue his daughter. Melville and his wife didn't talk about what happened, said nothing about the way the girl had stared. But Melville knew, had a sense already for what his wife was thinking. He knew that her days in public were nearing an end, that she was as certain as she needed to be about what the girl had seen in her. In the weeks that followed, before Melville stopped inviting his wife out of the house with him, before he became accustomed to her new sense of permanence, they said nothing about the girl whispering to her mother and pointing back at Melville's and his wife, accusing them of something.

Melville comes in through the front door while it's still night, but as the stars are beginning to lose their brightness. He comes into his cool, dark house where his wife is sleeping. He doesn't reach for the lights. He walks quietly up the stairs and down the long hallway to his bedroom. He thinks about waking his wife to tell her that for a few hours this morning it looks as though the sun and moon will share the same sky. He knows how she likes that all too common but still surprising event. He knows how she likes to look into the sky, how she likes not knowing why certain stars are brighter than others. Melville enters his bedroom and looks to where he left his wife sleeping only an hour or two earlier. The sheets are pulled back where he slept, but flat and almost smooth where his wife ought to be. He wonders where she might have gone at this hour. It isn't like her to wake in the night. He checks the bathroom but doesn't find her there.

He returns to the bed and moves in for a closer look, and he finds her, finally, where she had been all along. He was looking right at her, but he didn't see her. An easy mistake in the darkness. A simple trick of light that makes the sheet look flat when it isn't. She's there sleeping, breathing deeply. He's relieved to have found her, but only in that relief does he recognize the brief moment of panic that preceded it. It was foolish of him to react that way, he knows. He knows just as well that it won't be too much longer, not long at all, before this scene repeats itself with a slightly different ending.

The Tree of the Holy Virgin

A

We were told to expect aggressive behavior, including hair pulling. We were told that routine was important, and that some of the children would resist every effort we made to help them. We were cautioned against taking things personally.

B

The younger boys ran and played, and they loved to hide even if they lacked the patience to let us find them. The boy who ate enormously was incapable of speaking his own name.

C

There were hundreds of candles at the small city park across the street. The candles sat in glass cylinders printed with images of bleeding hearts, crucifixes, and saints, and they were set in rows at the base of the tree where Mary, the Virgin Mother, was said to have appeared.

D

Of the two cases of Down syndrome, one was classified moderate and the other extreme. We were told that one of these children was unable to use the bathroom by himself, and we were directed to use surgical gloves when assisting him.

E

Some of the children echoed nearly everything we said. They could answer questions with appropriate answers, but regularly they repeated our questions back at us. They also repeated dialogue from movies and television commercials they had seen hundreds of times.

F

Fungus grew from the woodchips in the fenced playground where the children played. The fungus looked like spilled chocolate milk, but we didn't notice it at first. When we did, it motivated us to move the children to the playground across the street where many people came daily to see the mark of the Virgin.

G

The girls had cerebral palsy, muscular dystrophy, speech delay, ADHD, and fragile X syndrome. One of the girls walked around saying: her dress, her shoes, her hat, her dress, her socks, her coat, her dress. Sometimes she said: her brassiere, and then giggled.

H

The hands that had touched the mark of the Virgin thousands of times had left it darkened and smooth. The oily decay of the mark had led some to sketch it or paint it. These representations were nailed above and below a knot in the tree where sap had dried and resembled the veiled figure of a woman.

I

All of the children were impaired. When pregnant mothers came to the park—with a frequency that surprised us—we supposed that they had come to visit the tree, hoping to escape complication and difficulty, hoping to escape impairment itself. But the pregnant mothers spent most of their time observing the children in our group.

J

The children wore jump ropes over their shoulders like oversized necklaces. There was a closet full of toys and supplies, and everything in it got used in a way we couldn't have expected. One of the girls helped us put puzzles back in their boxes every time the boys dumped the pieces on their heads.

K

We had kites but lacked an open field in which to fly them. We tried anyway, and left—at the end of the summer—a dozen or more stuck in the trees.

L

We had a Matthew, a Mark, and a John, but no Luke. We often wished that a new boy would join us to complete our gospels.

M

One child refused to participate in most of our activities. He preferred to watch movies, and would rewind the same fifteen seconds of tape over and over again. He cried when we locked the VCR away. He cried when we told him that he would have to do without movies for a while.

N

Someone brought a prie-dieu and set it at the base of the tree. A New Testament was left on the padded altar and got replaced each week as the current one began to show signs of wear. We were reminded that it was Friday when we noticed torn, folded, or crumpled pages. We noticed the way rain or drops of wax made it impossible for anyone to use the book.

O

The obese child always ate two lunches. He was the first to say thank you and would often do so in American Sign Language. He also knew how to sign toilet, paint, cat, and swim. We had to remind him to excuse himself when he burped.

P

We had dozens of bottles of tempura paint that we used daily. The children wore men's dress shirts backwards over their clothing and filled every inch of the butcher paper we placed in front of them. They raced to see who would be first to cover their paper. Eventually, we managed to decorate one long wall with these projects—each sheet of paper filled with the same black and brown mixture.

Q

When we asked the children to be quiet, to lower their voices from a shout or a scream, we could tell they didn't understand. We learned to distract them from their screaming as best we could.

R

We knew not to use the word retarded. The word made us uncomfortable, and this was, we said to each other, because we had only known it as a schoolyard taunt. But we heard the word on occasion and didn't know how to correct it.

S

Senior Citizens filled an assisted-living facility next to the park. The fire engines and ambulances that arrived several times weekly to care for or remove the elderly gave the children immeasurable delight. Yes, one of the boys would say, yes, yes, yes.

T

One child spent most of his time swinging on a tire suspended by heavy chains. He often slid from the tire, landing in the soft sand below, lying still and staring at the sky until we told him it was time to go.

U

We knew that one child was Mormon and another Catholic because their parents told us so, but we only knew about the Unitarian boy because of the T-shirts he wore.

V

There was always something more interesting to the children than the tree of the Virgin. Even as we admired the new artwork or that expanding field of candles, the children were drawn to a bird, or a stick, or the pieces of litter that had accumulated in the gutters.

W

Of the videos, the whale was a favorite. The whale sang opera—wanted to sing at the Met—but got harpooned by a zealous impresario bent on rescuing the opera singer he believed was trapped inside. After the story of the opera-singing whale came the story of the passive bull, and after the passive bull came the lion who thought he was sheep.

X

We kept track of when children arrived and when they left, which meals they were served and which they ate. An X meant that a child had missed a day or a meal and an opportunity to walk with us near the tree of the Holy Virgin.

Y

The children yelled and screamed often, and it was nearly impossible to decipher joy from pain. Even those who could articulate what they wanted began to yell and scream, and by the end of the summer we had become a very noisy group. The yelling and screaming were always accompanied by pointing, laughing, crying, or spinning in place.

Z

The last of our weekly field trips was to the zoo. Some of the children were disappointed when they saw how inactive the animals were. We left earlier than we had to, returned to the city park, and ate tuna fish sandwiches near the tree of the Holy Virgin.

The Hidden Curriculum

She looked at the papers in her lap and said that our son's homework record was—and she paused here—spotty. She said the word as though it were profane. We waited for her to explain what she meant. She said that our son had completed very little homework over the course of the school year up to this point. She continued to flip through pages until she reached the final page in her stack. It's possible, she said, that my records are wrong, but it appears that your son hasn't completed anything. Not that I can see, she said.

We looked at each other briefly, quizzically. Nothing at all? we asked.

She said that based on our reaction, she took it that our son was completing his homework but wasn't turning it in. Was this correct?

It's possible, we said.

You don't know?

We don't really believe in homework.

She nodded slowly, deliberately. I see, she said. Homework is an important part of what we do. There's clear evidence in numerous studies to show that homework done correctly and in the presence of a supervising parent is an important site of early cognitive development. It's crucial, it's absolutely crucial, that you help your son with his homework.

We nodded and smiled.

She began to say something but thought better of it. Then, as though it were a new idea altogether, she asked about reading. Your son reads well, she said. He's meeting his goals. He's on track to achieve his end-of-year targets, those established by the board of education. I take it you read with your son every day.

Sure, we said.

Do you? she asked, as though our first answer was somehow insufficient.

Sure, we said again, but this time with feeling.

She knew we meant well, she told us, but we needed to rethink our approach to our son's education. We needed to consider his long-term health and well-being. It was difficult, she told us, but with a little work it would begin to feel natural and normal. Second nature.

We agreed with her, saying that yes, our son's long-term well-being was, without question, without doubt, the most important thing. We said that we were prepared to do what we needed to do, that as his parents we were willing to make any sacrifice to help our son achieve the kind of balance and happiness that any parent would want for a child. Before we went further, we did have one question. We wanted to know if what our son had told us was true. Was it true that our son was forced to stand in the corner through long portions of the day, staring at the bricks there? Was this true?

Not wholly true, she said. Although yes, she did sometimes ask children to stand in the corner for very brief periods of time. We needed to understand that this was an important part of her system of order, a carefully planned and well-studied code of rules and repercussions.

We told her we didn't like it.

She said, We separate the child from the enjoyable experience of being with classmates, doing what classmates are doing. It's punishment by the removal of reward. It's very effective at teaching children the natural consequences of their decisions.

We said again that we didn't like it.

She said she understood, but that it was for the best, that it was all supported by the latest research. Our son, she said, had probably done certain things, had probably made certain decisions, had taken certain actions that qualified as minor infractions of the system of order, the repercussions of which were a specified though very limited number of minutes spent in the corner.

Probably? we asked. What did she mean when she said that our son had probably done things to get himself punished in this way?

Well, she said, I don't keep records of that kind of thing.

You should.

Yes, she said, but she didn't seem to mean it.

He's only six years old, we said.

Yes, she said, I'm aware.

And what about recess? we asked.

What about it?

We understand that you sometimes withhold recess as punishment.

Only very rarely, she said.

We don't like it, we said.

I understand, she said.

Our son loves recess. He loves nothing so much. In fact, if it weren't for recess, we aren't sure public education would have anything of value to offer him.

Yes, she said, physical education is an important part of what we do.

But you withhold it.

Only very rarely.

We'd like you to stop that.

She said she understood.

It's the running, we said. Have you seen our son run?

Yes, I believe I have.

It's his favorite thing. He's very good at it.

She said she wanted to ask about the food our son brought for lunch. As you know, she said, we discourage home lunch and would like very much for your son eat the food provided by the school and approved by the board of education. It would make things so much easier, she said, and it would do so much to improve your son's situation, his relationships with peers, his well-being, were you to allow him to eat the lunch the other children eat. It would do so much.

We said that we didn't like the options provided in the cafeteria, that we'd made a careful study of the menu and had found it lacking.

No, she said, it's very healthy.

Healthful, we corrected, and no it's not.

Yes, she said, the board of education has made it a top priority to guarantee that the food in our cafeteria is appropriate to the needs of our youngest learners. I can show you the report.

We don't need to see the report.

She watched us for a moment and then asked if this meant we were prepared to allow our son access to the same healthy or healthful menu of food options his peers were enjoying. Other parents, she said, were all too glad to have these meals provided for their children at a very reasonable cost.

We said that we intended to make no such change. There are hot dogs in the cafeteria, and we can't approve of hot dogs.

Is that it? she said.

Pizza, we said.

She watched us and waited.

And cake and cookies.

I see, she said. She looked at her lap, at the papers lying there. You would prefer your son to eat, am I saying this right, bulgur?

Yes, we said.

Every day? she said.

Yes, we said.

Plain? she said.

Sometimes, we said.

She looked at us and then at the papers. We anticipated her thought and explained that bulgur was a whole grain similar to cracked wheat and commonly used in Middle Eastern cuisines, particularly that of Turkey.

You want your son to eat it without a spoon or fork?

We find eating utensils wasteful.

We don't throw them out, she said, we wash them.

What about the water, we said? And the gas to heat that water? And the soap? And the equipment? And the labor?

She breathed deeply through her nose and said that it would be great if we would reconsider our insistence on home lunch. We smiled and nodded, indicating that we understood her obligation to say such things and that we were willing to wait patiently as she did so.

We've been working on some basic life skills as a class, she said, and your son does well in some areas, but not as well in others.

What others? we said.

Well, as an example, she said, he doesn't seem to know how to tie his shoelaces.

That makes sense, we said.

Right, but what I meant was that we were practicing shoe-tying as a class, and he didn't really seem to understand the concept.

Of course, we said. And there's a reason for that. Please understand, we see the knot of a shoelace, and really any knot for that matter, irrespective of the ease with which it might be undone or untied, as a metaphor.

A metaphor? she said.

Yes, we said, we oppose knots of all sorts.

She tilted her head at this, waiting as though for some process to run its course.

For his long-term well-being, we said.

She kept her head tilted as it had been. She licked her lips. She cleared her throat. She said, He doesn't wear shoes at all, not even slip-ons or flip-flops. You know, a great many students in my classes have trouble tying a shoelace because, like your son, they've never had to. Which is fine, but they do wear shoes, just of another sort, the kind with buckles or Velcro straps, for example. There are many shoes without laces.

We said we understood.

In fact, she said, we have reason to believe that your son may have a touch of frostbite on his toes.

His toe, we corrected, it's just the one and it's not frostbite. It might look that way, we said, but it's not frostbite. He'll be fine. In fact, his feet will be stronger for it, more resistant. He's building calluses now that will serve him well throughout his life. He has strong feet.

Her head was no longer tilted, and she stared at us as though we were obligated to say more.

There are people in Kenya, we said, and in Ghana, and really all throughout Africa, who never wear shoes. There are marathon runners who have never worn shoes. The human foot wasn't meant to be shod. It damages the structure of the foot tremendously, forcing a person to distribute his weight incorrectly. It's bad for the foot, the leg, the back. Say goodbye to good posture. His feet are strong and getting stronger. You should see how well he runs. He's a very fine runner.

Yes, she said, you mentioned that, but it does look like frostbite.

It isn't, we said, and it's really very minor.

Were there questions we wanted to ask? Did we have concerns? Because now was the time.

We want an end of crepe paper, we said, and finger paint too. The toxins, we said, we won't have it.

There are no toxins, she said.

We told her we begged to differ.

It's state policy, she said. The board of education has given the mandate. Look. She pulled a box of crayons from a crate near her feet. See, she said, non-toxic, it's printed right here.

Oh no, we said.

What? she said.

You don't know?

I don't understand. You were concerned about toxicity, and I've told you that there are no toxins in this classroom as per board of education mandate, and these crayons are one clear example.

We watched her say this. We waited for her to realize how foolish she sounded.

What? she said.

The talc? we said. The paraffin? Just think of the toll. Just think of the long-term cost of that one box, we said.

The cost? she said.

Yes, we said, and we asked her to please include crayons on the list of things that she was to stop using immediately.

What's left? she said. If we don't have crepe paper and we don't have paint and we don't have crayons, what do you expect us to do all day?

There's running, we said.

Yes, she said. I'll see about increasing the amount of running we do.

You don't have to run, we said. It's fine with us if you let him run alone. You don't have to be with him.

Thank you, she said. She would consider our recommendations.

We thanked her.

Was there anything else, she wanted to know.

No, we said, we didn't think so. More recess, we said, just that.

Yes, she said. She had made a note.

We said we were pleased to know that our son was a priority for her.

She stood and reached to shake our hands. We said good-bye and walked across that hard and colorful carpet, past the letters of the alphabet displayed on the wall. We saw ourselves out of the room and walked down the tiled hallway. We nodded at the custodian with his floor-buffing machine, the ground dull and flat before him, shiny and smooth in the long stretch behind him. We walked past the nurse's office, the music room, the library. We walked beneath the exit sign, through the double doors with their wire-reinforced glass. We walked outside where the grass needed mowing but felt so nice and so cool.

In California

T*hat was the year our sister died.* She was four years old and was never supposed to have a long life, but that hardly changed anything. Dad said she wasn't like other disabled children, which was a way of defending rather than excusing her handicap. When we saw Down syndrome kids at the park—their faces puffy, their lips cracked, their eyes too far apart—he told us that some kids were born with birth defects and that it was sad. Amy, on the other hand, this sister of ours, simply hadn't developed like she was supposed to. Her brain, he said, was just a little too small, just a little less than it ought to be. Even then, as boys with no grasp of genetics or heredity, we knew that what Dad said was only partly true. We had watched Amy and could see that in many ways she was just like the other handicapped kids at the playground, and just like the other kids in her school, which wasn't really a school at all.

That was the year we had a swimming pool we never used. Mom explained that it wasn't so easy as turning on the hose and filling it up, that there were chemicals we needed to put in the water to keep it clean, and expensive equipment to buy. She also said that the crack in the bottom of the pool looked small but that it was enough for the water to leak into the ground. We spent the better part of one afternoon poking pencils and sewing needles through the bottoms of Dixie cups as she demonstrated her point. Once she had us convinced, she promised that she would talk to Dad and have him call a repair company. At first, when we reminded her that the crack was still there and suggested that Dad maybe needed to call the company again, she said she would make sure he did. But when we moved back to Utah that August, the crack was still there.

That was the year we fought about everything. We were only boys, Dad said, and we were only doing what brothers naturally did. Mom said she couldn't understand it. She couldn't understand how one of us managed to care about a toy only when the other began to play with it. She couldn't understand why we couldn't keep our hands to ourselves, why we couldn't go five minutes without hitting each other, why we felt this need to argue about the most meaningless things. High up in the pantry, on a shelf we couldn't reach even with a footstool, she kept of box of toys we had fought over. She promised to return those toys when we calmed down and agreed to play nicely, but we knew that if a toy went into that box, we weren't likely to get it back anytime soon.

That was the year I turned eight and David turned six. If we saw someone we hadn't seen in a while, an aunt or uncle or an old family friend, that person would look at us for a few seconds and say to Mom and Dad that they couldn't believe how big we were getting. They never said it to us directly, but they always said it. Sometimes, when we were introduced to people for the first time, they would grab hold of our biceps and pretend to be surprised by our enormous strength. When they turned their attention to Amy, however, they said how beautiful she was, just like a normal girl. Mom and Dad always smiled at that, but we knew it bothered them.

That was the year our house was filled with safety latches. Every cupboard and every door was locked. Dad said the latches were there to protect Amy from herself. She had busy hands, he said, and she didn't always know how to control them. She never learned to walk, but Dad said she hardly needed to since she moved fast enough on her hands and knees. Sometimes she scooted herself along in a seated position and we would do the same. She loved this game and giggled when we played it. She also loved to hide from us while we tried to find her. We pretended we couldn't see her when she covered her eyes or when she buried her head into Dad's chest. She laughed every time we said, Where's Amy? Where did Amy go?

That was the year we had superhero drinking glasses. The glasses were gifts from Katie, our babysitter. She got them from a fast-food restaurant where she worked part-time. Katie called that restaurant her day job and said the glasses were part of a promotion but that nobody minded if she took one or two for us. It wasn't long before we had the complete set of ten. Only a couple of those glasses made it through the year, though. Most of them ended up in the kitchen garbage after one of us boys or Dad dropped them on the yellow linoleum floor or in the sink. Each time Mom heard one of those glasses fall and break, she sighed heavily and said, Oh, Katie, as if Katie had been the one to drop it. Mom was always the one to sweep the shards and small slivers of glass into the dustpan because, she said, there was Amy to think about and she couldn't trust any of the men in the house to do a thorough job. After Amy died, Mom was still the one to do the sweeping up, but then she said it was because she wanted to feel safe in bare feet.

That was the year Dad built airplanes for the Army. He left on his ten-speed bicycle every morning at eight and came home at five-thirty. He wore a Velcro strap around the cuff of his right leg so the fabric of his pants wouldn't get caught in the chain. At night, he sketched pictures of airplanes for us and sometimes he brought home books filled with photographs of those jets and bombers and cargo transports. It was years before we understood that Dad was as far removed from the actual airplanes as anyone could be, but at the time we imagined him tightening nuts and bolts and testing out the controls in the cockpit. It also took years for us to understand how much Dad disliked his work, how dissatisfied he was, and how he felt trapped between the job he hated and the war that job kept him from fighting.

That was the year we wore three-piece suits and clip-on ties to church. The sleeves were too long and the legs too short, but Mom said we looked like little gentlemen. During church we counted the pockets on our vests and pretended we were secret agents with some clever device hidden in every fold. Mom hushed us when we argued or fought and Dad said it wasn't okay to bring guns to church, not even pretend guns we made with our hands. So, we turned to pencils and paper and made mazes for each other. Sometimes Dad drew incomplete pictures like the head of an elephant or the wheels of a car and then asked us to finish them. Sometimes he showed us how to fold paper airplanes but made us promise not to fly them until we were outside.

That was the year we wore our suits to Amy's funeral. We didn't play games then and we didn't draw. We sat quietly and listened as first one and then another of the people from our church stood to talk about the blessing Amy had been. They talked about how enthusiastic she always was, how energetic. They talked about how much happier they were when she was in the room. They said that God had special ways and special plans and that it was hard to know just how he was going to bless us, but that this little girl was nothing short of a miracle. We had heard some of these things before, but mostly we heard other things. We heard the parents of other handicapped children, at Amy's school, or at the playground, talk about how difficult it was to do the most basic things anymore. It was hard, they said, and Mom or Dad nodded and said they knew all about it. We often heard Mom say how impossible it was to keep Amy healthy, that she was always catching one thing or another. At the funeral, Dad was the last to stand and speak. He thanked everyone and said how these last months had been the most difficult he had ever known, but that he was grateful for the support our family had received. He said that at the end, he stayed awake and held her every night. He held her in his lap, he said, as she coughed and struggled to sleep. A night or two before she died, he knew it was almost over. He said he knew he had to let her go because it was time and she simply couldn't hold on any longer. But he hadn't been ready, he said, and he hadn't been willing.

That was the year Mom cried and cried. At first, she would hide herself away in her bedroom, doing her best to make excuses, saying she had something in her eye or that her allergies were unbearable, but it wasn't long before we found her at the kitchen sink, peeling vegetables for dinner, her eyes red and her cheeks smeared with moisture she had wiped at but not wiped away. When we asked what was wrong, worried that maybe we were responsible for all the crying even though we hadn't been fighting, Mom bent down to hug us, wrapping one arm around David and one arm around me, squeezing us tightly. I asked her what was wrong and if maybe we were in trouble. She looked at me as if I had said something startling, then took my face in her hands, wiped with her thumb at something under my eyes, and brushed the hair back from my forehead. She smiled then, like she was proud of what she had done to me, like she had prepped me for a school photograph. She looked at me as if she wanted to say something but didn't have the words. I saw the skin around her mouth tighten and relax once and then twice. Then she made a sound that wasn't quite a word and pulled us into her chest where I could feel what crying did to her body.

That was the year neighbors brought us more food than we could eat. They brought casseroles and homemade bread and pie. All the food came with little cards that Mom opened and read and stacked up on the kitchen table. Many afternoons, we found her writing thank-you notes on cards that looked just like the others. Sometimes, when a note she was writing was to a neighbor we knew well or the parents of our friends or when the food was something we boys had especially liked, Mom would ask us to write our names on the note as well. In big, blocky letters that nearly filled the cards, we wrote Love David and Love James.

That was the year Christmas was warm and snowless. We both found a set of Legos under the tree but wasted no time combining them into one big pile. We also found candy, new clothes, and a slot-car racing set Dad played with more than we did. He joked that maybe Santa hadn't meant it for us and that maybe this was the set he had asked for but never got when he was a kid. After the presents were opened and we had begun to wear out, Mom and Dad sat us down and said they had one more present. It wasn't a present exactly, they said, but something to be excited about. They asked how we would feel about having a new baby in the family. We were thrilled, of course, and talked about how much fun it would be. Mom said the baby was on its way, but that it would be a while still before it was ready to leave her belly. In the meantime, she said, the baby could probably hear us if we wanted to whisper to it. So, we leaned in close and said, Hello baby, hello baby.

That was the year we ate Kentucky Fried Chicken on the beach. On holidays and sometimes just because, Dad would ask if maybe we didn't want to get out of the house and take advantage of life in Southern California. Dad wore pants and socks and a wide-brimmed hat that cast a long shadow over his face. He and Mom never wore swimsuits or got very near the water, but they let us run in the foamy waves as long as David promised to stay close to me and I promised to stay where they could see us. Mom wondered how sand managed to get everywhere, even on her chicken, and said that she would like the beach better if it weren't so dirty. Dad smiled and said that was a good one, but Mom shrugged as if to say she wasn't joking. Sometimes we walked together through the sand or on the sidewalk above the beach and watched the sun set. We went hunting for sand dollars or starfish but except for small, broken seashells, we rarely found more than seaweed and aluminum cans.

That was the year Mom rubbed her stomach like a worry stone. The last thing we saw every morning as we left for school was Mom standing in the doorway, waving goodbye with one hand and rubbing her stomach with the other. Most days we found her there when we returned, hours later. It was easy to imagine that she stood that way all day long, that while we were saying the Pledge of Allegiance or learning the multiplication tables, or while we ran and played at recess, she stood on the front porch of our small home moving her hands up and down, up and down. When we asked questions about the baby, Mom sat us down and explained what it was going to be like. It was going to be hard work, she said, because babies needed a lot of attention, and they cried all the time, and she needed all the help we could give. She said it was important that we be gentle with the baby and careful not to roughhouse around it. We asked what we were going to name the baby and if it would be a boy or a girl. Mom said we'd have to wait and see.

That was the year Mom and Dad went to the hospital and Aunt Val stayed with us. When Mom and Dad left, they took Mom's orange and green hospital suitcase with them, the one that had been sitting in the closet for weeks. They said Aunt Val was going to be a lot of fun but that we had to promise to be extra good for her and help clean the kitchen and do all of our homework without being asked. Most importantly, they said, we were not to argue with Aunt Val about any-thing. We promised to do everything we were supposed to do and hugged and kissed them both goodbye. When we said we were excited and couldn't wait to see the new baby, Dad smiled and said he was excited too, but Mom turned and walked down the porch steps and didn't look back at us or say anything. We watched them all the way to the car, but even then, as Dad was backing out, Mom didn't look at us or wave goodbye. Aunt Val made pancakes for breakfast both mornings Mom and Dad were gone, and one night she let us stay up late enough to watch M*A*S*H.

That was the year Mom didn't have a baby. When she came home from the hospital, holding onto Dad's arm all the way from the car to the front door, she had her orange and green suitcase, but her stomach wasn't as big and there was no baby. Aunt Val was the first to hug Mom while we stood and waited. Mom didn't say anything, but Aunt Val said she was so, so sorry. Aunt Val cried but Mom didn't, and they stood that way for a long time, not talking. Finally, Dad pulled us into the kitchen because he said he had a surprise for us. The surprise turned out to be candy he'd bought at the hospital gift shop, but when he knelt down to give it to us, he said he had some bad news. He said that the baby, a girl, was what they called a stillborn. That meant she was with God, he said. That meant she was dead. When we asked if there was going to be a funeral for the baby, Dad looked at us like he hadn't even thought about it. He said he didn't know, and then he said he didn't think so.

That was the year we learned about unborn babies. We learned that before a baby is born it gets its food through a tube and that if anything happens to that tube—if it gets twisted or pinched in certain ways—the baby simply starves to death or suffocates. The baby that would have been our second sister was just too active, Mom said. She twisted and turned until she finally pinched that tube and no food could get through it. We didn't understand all the details, but Mom said that she didn't either. She also said that she was through with crying, that she would never cry again. She said it like a joke, as if it was supposed to be funny, and we knew that she wasn't serious, but we didn't see her cry again for a long time. For weeks after, Dad spent a lot of time at home both in the mornings and in the afternoons. He was the one who sent us off to school most of those days. If he wasn't home when we returned, he was still home earlier than we were used to. In time, he went back to his old schedule and Mom, once again, was the one waving goodbye from the porch each morning.

That was the year Dad pounded a For Sale sign into our front lawn. The first person to look at the house was a tall man with a thick, dark mustache. He said he had boys just like us, but when he came inside, he kept talking about which rooms would be good for his dogs and which would not. After he left, David asked Mom where we were going to sleep if the man put his dogs in our bedroom. Mom laughed at that and said we didn't need to worry about the dogs, that we would be long gone by the time they moved in. I asked where we were going, and she said that Dad had found a better job in Utah and that we were moving back.

That was the year we packed our clothes and toys into boxes. Dad let us help as he loaded those boxes into a moving truck. Dad drove the truck and we went in the car with Mom. While we drove, we watched for license plates and freeway signs out the window to see who could find the letters of the alphabet most quickly. We did word searches in big books Mom had bought just for the trip and ate pretzels and cookies until we were sick of them. We stopped at McDonald's in Las Vegas where we ate Happy Meals. Mom asked what we thought about all this traveling and if we were having fun. We said we were even if we were tired of the car already and didn't want to get back in. It was seven or eight hours later when we got to Salt Lake City. We drove through streets we had never seen before and ended up at a house that was not our house. We must have looked disappointed because Mom asked what was wrong. When we asked whose house this was, she smiled and said it was ours. We said it wasn't our house because ours was white not brown and didn't have pine trees in front. Mom stopped smiling then and looked as tired as she had ever been. She sighed deeply before getting out of the car. She said we needed to hurry up. She said she needed us to be good boys.

The Weather Here

When Mandelbaum doesn't return for what must be days, we assume the worst. Although we haven't reached a consensus on what the worst might be, we're collectively relieved that for the first time in memory, no one is saying anything about Doppler radar. Since Mandelbaum was the one most likely to disagree on any subject, his absence gives some relief. We've considered that he may have left for good as he's long promised, but he said all sorts of things and what reason do we have to take him at his word now? What we know is that for the moment he's gone, and we don't miss his complaints.

We've become expert prognosticators in our time, and we like to congratulate one another for this talent. It's our unique ability, we're sure, to anticipate the future. We've successfully predicted many things and will continue to do so. We won't have food again tomorrow, we say, and we're right. We won't sleep and can only vaguely remember ever having done so, and again we're unanimous. It will rain tomorrow, we're sure. We have no precise means of measuring days, but the fleas come at day-like intervals. When they do, we have no recourse but to lie in the mud and wait for them to move on.

It's hopeless for us to waste our energies, so we return to what we know best. Tanner removes himself and pounds away at blocks of concrete that are slowly revealing themselves to be symbols of some sort. With these and a host of other rocks, he's preparing to explain to us, in graphic form, why it's possible though not likely that the rain will subside. It's likely to rain tomorrow, Tanner tells us, but there's a ten percent chance it won't. Look, he says. He's found a stick somewhere and uses it to point at the rocks. Perhaps this is too much for us to make sense of, he says. He sits down in a puddle and sets to work again. In time everything will become clear.

We can't see the sun, but we aren't convinced it's absent. To be fair, we can't see much of anything, and the darkness here is something we struggle with. We'd like to believe that the rain clouds above are simply thick enough to block sunlight, but some have begun to question whether we ever had a sun in the first place. When Villagran mentions the sun, he's started to use his fingers as quotation marks, reminding the rest of us that he was the first to theorize that the sun may never have existed. Isn't it possible, Villagran asks us, that the sun is just an idea we've talked ourselves into?

We have walls but no roofs. Mandelbaum called this place a ruin. He said the broken stones were evidence that something better had once been here, but that things had gone to pieces. We didn't share his confidence that the presence of crumbling walls necessitated the history of something better. We've hypothesized that this had been the site of good intentions not yet completed. Like Mandelbaum, we've wished for a roof over our heads, protection from the elements, but we don't share his opinions on much else. These walls are what we know, and we like them well enough. We see no reason to wander off aimlessly, looking for something better. We're willing to wait things out. Once the rain stops, we'll be in a better position to make improvements.

Orton and Halston are standing shoulder-to-shoulder, faces turned to the sky while rain pours over them. Halston wants to know if Orton knows the difference between partly cloudy and partly sunny. The rain hits Halston's face with force, his eyes blinking fiercely. Orton's eyes are closed. Of course he knows the difference, Orton says, does Halston take him for a fool? Yes, Halston says, he does take Orton for a fool, because he knows, as Orton obviously does not, that there's no difference between partly cloudy and partly sunny. Semantics, Halston says, that's your difference. Ah, Orton says, but you've forgotten that it can be partly cloudy at night but never partly sunny. And here, Halston says, what would you say we have here? Orton doesn't open his eyes to say that we have rain. You see my point then, Halston says, you see that I'm right and you're misleading yourself? No, Orton says, I see only rain.

It was Mandelbaum's contention that all of us here are dead. He was wrong, of course, and we proved it to him a dozen ways. Will a dead man complain about fleas that won't stop biting him? Will a dead man talk to other dead men? Will a dead man make predictions about the weather? Of course, he wouldn't hear these arguments. He couldn't remember eating or sleeping or whether he had a family, and these things were proof enough, he told us. We took it as our task to convince him that he was wrong and that his failing memory was no justification. He was alive, we told him, because his hair was still growing and his fingernails. He was alive because his teeth ached. More importantly, he was alive because he had the capacity to consider that he might not be. Dead men don't wonder if they're dead. Dead men know exactly what they are. Mandelbaum said only that if this was life, he didn't care to live it.

Fitzpatrick is convinced that the rain is coming to an end. He cites, as evidence, the lack of foliage and ground cover. This much rain can only exist in a lush and tropical ecosystem, he tells us. The lack of greenery suggests that it's rained for too long, that the ecosystem has lost its balance. These things correct themselves, he says. In time, these things always correct themselves. Villagran calls Fitzpatrick a buffoon and tells him that no one has ever said so much that came to so little. You're absolutely and exactly wrong, Villagran says. He says that rain creates an environment in which flora can thrive. Hollinger agrees with Fitzpatrick and Villagran enough to say that he too anticipates the end of rain, but he fears that drought will follow. There will be a period, he says, that's as dry as this one is wet. Hollinger asks how long it's been raining. We have no answer, but we agree that it's been a while. It's been raining for as long as we can remember. And how long is that? he asks. What can we say but that we can't remember anything we can't remember. Exactly, Hollinger says, as though he has proven a point. Hollinger's logic is not so convincing as we hoped it might be, but we're less concerned with logic than we are with conviction. We tell him we see his point, and that it's a good one. Except Fitzpatrick. Fitzpatrick says, No, no, no, no. Fitzpatrick says he can't agree with a flimsy argument based on nothing. It's useless, he says, to assume that this rain has come to us without cause. And that cause, he says, is the plow. The plow? Hollinger says. What plow? Can you please show me a plow? My point, Fitzpatrick says, is that this ground has been turned and made ready for rain. This rain is a natural response to that preparation. A tilled soil draws the rain, he says. It's circular, he says. You must recognize the circularity. We say that yes, we would like to recognize a circularity.

Wait, Hollinger says. What are you talking about? Why must we admit to your logic? Why must we agree with you before you've proven anything? That's just the point, Fitzpatrick says, I've already proven everything. And with that we applaud Fitzpatrick. We admire his cunning. We cheer his name, in the rain, waiting for the ecosystem to correct itself.

We find it odd that while the rain seems to remain constant, we're sometimes able to speak at conversational levels, but just as often, we have to yell to be heard. Tanner is most disturbed by these changes because his voice is so soft. He tells us, when he can, that the problem is one of focus, and that we would hear him quite clearly if we made half an effort. The rain is louder, Tanner says, when we allow it to be. This sort of explanation is exactly the kind of thing that gets Halston all worked up. It's Halston's opinion that we are incapable of enacting change, and that acceptance is the only path. The rain, he argues, is constant, and it does no good to look for minute distinctions one moment to the next. Our position, he says, is fixed, and the sooner we accept it the better. Tanner wants to know why it is, if our position is so helpless, that Halston is always the last one running around when the fleas come, why he refuses to simply let them do what they will do.

Mandelbaum spoke so often of Doppler radar that we began to fear for his sanity. While it's true, as he often said, that a little technology can go a very long way, we weren't prepared to spend our days waiting for a radar system that can only tell us what we already know. What we know is rain, and what good is technology that simply names the obvious? Rain is rain, we told Mandelbaum, and we need no technology to establish that fact. Mandelbaum said that there was something more than rain and that he was going to find it. He said he couldn't stand the fleas any longer.

The fleas come in enormous waves that cover the ground completely. They come by the millions and cover every inch of our bodies until we're so thoroughly bitten that nothing remains for them to bite. We've tried to hide, or run, or cover ourselves, but the fleas move quickly. We've come to an odd sort of respect for their timing. They're capable, these little fiends, of avoiding the rain that so thoroughly drenches us, and they know just how often to return, just when our itching blisters have begun to recede. Villagran suggests we take a lesson from the fleas, that we find a means by which to avoid the rain by keeping on the move. We've made attempts at Villagran's plan but have only made ourselves tired and hot, soaked through by rain and sweat. Fitzpatrick and Tanner were never convinced that such a plan could work in the first place because we are, they thought, too large and too slow as men. What we need, they both said, is a roof. Villagran hasn't stopped running, though, and although he looks tired most of the time, we think he might be getting a little faster.

Tanner suggests that it's perhaps our lack of historical context making things so difficult. He proposes making a list of the things we remember and can agree on. He's convinced that only through consensus will we ever achieve anything worthwhile, and for once he speaks so loudly that we find it hard to disagree. So we begin. We have no means of writing since not even mud at our feet will hold its shape, but we feel confident we can create verbal consensus. Orton remembers the last wave of fleas and how they made it difficult for him to walk. Halston remembers rain and nothing else. Hollinger remembers Mandelbaum and his longing for certain technologies. Villagran remembers the phrase "low-pressure zone," but he can't make sense of it. Tanner remembers his clothing when it was more than the rags it is now. Fitzpatrick remembers a time when he thought the rain was ending. We agree that we have the sense of a time before the rain but not one of us can form a clear memory. We agree that Mandelbaum has been gone for quite a while now, and that his return, which once seemed imminent, feels less likely the longer we think about it. It turns out we agree on a lot of things, but then Orton wants to know if he's the only one who remembers making this list before.

Fitzpatrick says that his knee no longer hurts. He'd given up on his hope for an end to the rain, but this is something to believe in. His knee, he says, is never wrong. Halston finds it odd that Fitzpatrick hasn't mentioned his knee before if he's willing to invest so much in it now. For his part, Fitzpatrick can't remember mentioning his knee either but he's sure he must have because it always bothers him. His knee, he says, hurts when the rain is coming, and the fact that it's hurt for so long has always meant that more rain was on the way. But now, he says, now his knee is pain-free and that's new and that means he has something to work with. The rain is coming to an end, Fitzpatrick says, and the proof is in my joints. Wait a minute, Halston says, wait a minute, are you sure it ever didn't hurt before? Are you even sure which knee it was? Fitzpatrick is sure, so very sure, so completely sure that the pain was in his left knee, and so what if he's limping a bit, so what if his elbow hurts? His left knee feels great and that should count for something.

Mandelbaum liked the idea of punishment. He said that we should at least consider the possibility of judgment, that we should give some thought to things we did before we got to where we are. He said we had probably said and done unforgivable things and that this place was a consequence of those actions. He said we needed the rain to cleanse us, that it was a metaphor for something, and that the fleas were a metaphor, too, but that he couldn't be sure for what. He said we needed to find some answers to some questions and that

Doppler radar was going to provide those answers because when had it ever steered us wrong? When had modern technology ever been less than what we needed? He said that we were being punished for misdeeds and that our pasts were catching up to us. He said that this place was the opposite of a resting place, that it was a restless place in which we could not find peace. He also believed there was an end to this place, that we might learn something from it and get through it.

Things aren't as bad as Mandelbaum would have us believe. Still, we sometimes wish he were here. We can't help but feel that his contrariness was important somehow. We can't help but hope that even now he's returning from some far-off place to tell us again about our just rewards and to explain what the rain means and what it's trying to teach us. We imagine him there, just beyond the horizon. He's coming back with an apology or a petition for our pity. He's going to say he's sorry for leaving and glad to be back. We're happy to wait. After all, when we set our minds to it, we agree that things are not so bad, that the fleas are fine if they get what they want, and that the rain is hardly as heavy as it could be. Our skin is never dry, we're rarely thirsty, and the mud feels good between our toes and in our hands. We can wait here as long as it takes. We don't mind. We've got nowhere to be.

Maybe the Kids Maybe

A *fat man runs up* and then down their street in a gray sweat suit and striped headband. The husband laughs because it's funny, he says, the way the fat man runs, like he's pushing up against some impossible force, his weight too much for his strength. The wife says how strange it is, that this man has kept it up, that his running has gone on longer than expected, that it has been weeks when she, for one, was sure he would quit after days. The wife says that the fat man's efforts have made him seem stronger and more determined, or at least more persistent, than she gave him credit for. The husband says it's only a matter of perception, and that this man is still only a fat man, sweating through a threadbare sweat suit, looking ridiculous.

They sit on opposite ends of the same couch and watch one of their favorite cooking shows. The episode is dedicated to desserts from around the world. They see cream and sugar and chocolate in a dozen shapes, combined with the most unusual things: fruits they've never heard of and something that looks like ash or charcoal. Most of all they see obscene amounts of butter. The host gets very serious when he explains that there's no substitute for butter, that margarine or shortening or lower fat oils are all guarantees of lost flavor. The husband and the wife look at each other like they didn't see this coming, like they never thought, after so many years of being told to avoid fatty foods, that they would hear butter described so reverently. It's right at that moment that the show cuts to a commercial for weight loss pills. It's one they've seen before, but it seems strange now. The host of the cooking show was just telling them to eat more butter and then this commercial promises weight loss on one pill a day. It's strange, the husband says. Yes, the wife says, it really is.

The husband says that he sometimes wonders what it means to be fat, what it feels like. He knows enough about spare tires and double chins, about holiday weight and winter layers, but he doesn't really know obesity. He sees this man running past his house and he wonders what that much weight will do to one's knees. He wonders how the fat man manages it, putting that much weight in motion. He sees him as a cautionary tale, as proof that one's health is not to be taken for granted. But he also sees him as an example of what his sister said when she called last week, when she mentioned a new study she'd just read. She said that no one over the age of thirty should run for exercise. She said that this study had it all right there in clinical research, that running did irreparable damage to joints and muscles. She said that runners were increasingly at risk as they grew older.

Full figures, of course, were once a sign of wealth. They have seen the paintings in museums and in history books. They have seen them, in fact, in the very books their children bring home from school. So many pages dedicated to enormous monarchs. The wife wonders about the relationship between obesity and wealth, thinness and poverty. The commercials on television trouble her. She can't help but turn away, she says, from those images of starving children in Africa and South America, their arms and legs as thin as twigs, their bellies distended by something other than indulgence. She can't bear it, she says. She feels manipulated by the false sincerity of Hollywood stars. She knows that the suffering is real, but she also knows that someone other than those poor children will profit from her donation. She knows that starvation will continue with or without her money. She changes the channel and finds coverage of strong men yoked to train cars, pulling those loads like oxen. Just look at that, she says. Isn't that something?

The fat man runs up the street and they expect to see him thinning. But he doesn't. He goes on sweating, goes on with his labored breathing, and doesn't seem to benefit one bit from his efforts. They've heard somewhere that weight is built into human genes. The evidence suggests that a fat man will always be a fat man unless he starves himself, and a thin man must gorge himself to put on significant weight. They have heard that adopted children mimic their biological parents' weight patterns more than those of their adopted parents. You see, the husband says to the wife. Isn't this proof that nature wins? Or that this fat man can exhaust himself and get nowhere? What it means, the wife says, is that we have half a gallon of ice cream in the freezer and there's no reason not to eat it.

When they talk, they say things they've always said and hardly notice their own metaphors. They say, for example, that people who matter are heavyweights, while a lightweight is useless. They talk about heavy hitters who have enacted change or who have made consequential decisions. They talk about the heavies who occupy the television screen: mafia thugs and arch-villains. If weight is also something to lament—as when they criticize those who are heavy-handed—they still spend much of their attention on those misuses of power and influence. To be weighty is to be of value, to be worth their time and attention. They admire bigwigs and ignore small fries. As they look through their kitchen window and watch the fat man running by, they wonder how they feel about him. They wonder if they ought to respect him.

At the dinner table, one of their daughters talks about compressed stars called white dwarfs and says that a spoonful of one would weigh several thousand pounds in our gravity. The husband says he wonders what they might do with a spoonful of anything that weighed as much as a car. He wonders how something so dense and heavy could be put to use by the strong men on television or how one might use such a spoonful in a practical joke. The daughters laugh at this and imagine what fun it would be to slip some white dwarf into a friend's backpack or into someone's shoe. Yes, says the wife. If we had just one teaspoon of white dwarf imagine the fun we might have.

They're concerned when their daughters, gathered at the kitchen table as they often are, notice the fat man running up and down the street. It's not only that they see him because the girls might also see a moral in that man, but that other ideas could be creeping inside their heads. Their daughters who are just now coming into young adulthood. What must they think when they see this man working so hard to accomplish so little? They have heard about anorexia and bulimia and wonder if such disorders are already at work inside them. They're still very young, of course, but they worry about things they can't control. What are they hearing from friends? What are they seeing online? Every time they see the fat man struggling up the street, their daughters seem, if possible, a sliver more narrow than they were before.

Their son, too, spends time at the kitchen window as the fat man goes by. He's only twelve, and they know that his life has been defined by his sisters. He rarely goes outside where other boys are often playing ball games of one sort or another. He spends too much time in his room, ordering and reordering various collectibles: ribbons for academic excellence, books that have survived the girls and books of his own, action figures of mythological beasts, seashells, and sand dollars found on one or another of their family vacations. Sometimes, at the sight of him, they catch their breath. Like his sisters, he seems too thin. He complains, too, of being tired all the time. For the while, they thought his growth was simply outpacing his appetite, but they wonder if that's it. They ask each other what they should do. The husband says that it might be time to say something. The wife says it probably wouldn't hurt to sit down and talk about it.

They see a program on television in which an obese man consults with doctors about his life-threatening condition. The doctors say the man's body doesn't know when it has enough food. The man could literally eat himself to death and never feel full. They tell him that a medication would help with the condition, but that they have to get his weight down and fast. The man's body is a ticking bomb; surgery is the only option. The husband and the wife wonder if these doctors are really doctors. This is television, after all. They must know that their advice is making its way into homes around the world. The husband says that it's wrong for the doctors to frighten the man the way they do, using this language of bombs. The wife says that what's worse is the lack of willpower they assume in their patient. Wouldn't this operation effectively force the man to lose weight? What he needs, she says, is a sense of empowerment and a sense of accomplishment. What this man needs, she says, is emotional support.

There's nothing they can do to ensure their children will respect their rules or take their advice. The husband and the wife have read books on parenting and most agree that teenagers can't help but see their parents as unenlightened buffoons. Some of the books say that hard rules should be avoided, that teenage children need broad moral landscapes. The husband says he isn't sure what that means, but he thinks he disagrees. Where the books do agree is in their assessment of former generations of parents. About those parents from decades ago, the books might say they meant well or that they were doing the best they could, but they insist that the tools and techniques and disciplinary approaches of those generations must be avoided. The wife says that the writers of these books can't mean to confuse us, but she finds them baffling. Can it be true, she says, that our parents got so much wrong?

They watch their son standing at the kitchen window, watching the fat man running. The boy is too thin, and the man is too fat, and the husband whispers that now is as good a time as any. The wife says no and pulls the husband into another room. She's been thinking, she says, about something she heard just last week on radio editorial about how parents plan too much for their children. The editorial was given by a mother who encouraged parents to reconsider the value of averages and said that children reading at their own grade level are not failures but are where they should be. The mother argued that so many soccer practices and play rehearsals and music classes and after-school programs did not prepare children for success but assured failure. She said that children needed unstructured time. She also said that parents needed to spend more time with their children and less time driving their children. There was a pun there: driving and driving, but it was true more than it was funny. The husband stands there, not sure what to think. Their son doesn't know he's being watched while he stares at the fat man. After a minute, the husband says his gut says they should say something, that talking is better than not talking.

Before the wife can remind the husband that this isn't his decision alone, their son moves from the window, walks down the hallway, and slips quietly into his room.

The husband says he heard last week about this man who, at eighty-six, had run ninety-nine marathons. It was one of those news stories, he says, that they save for the last minute or so of the hour, the kind of news that isn't so much news as antidote for all that precedes it. This man was the picture of health, the reporters said, absolutely sound in mind and body. The husband says he hadn't paid much attention to the story at the time and that he would have forgotten about the old marathon runner if he hadn't seen him in the news again just a day or two later. As it turns out, the man never made it to his one-hundredth marathon. He had a heart attack while jogging near his home. The husband read of the death in the paper where they told the story like it was still good news, as though this man was a model for the rest of us. Couldn't we make the argument that running is what killed the man? Couldn't I make the case, the husband says, that while this man may have lived a long life, he didn't prove anything definitively? These reporters would have us believe that this man lived longer because of running, that his focus on health made him a better person, but we don't know that. Who's to say that all that running didn't put undue strain on his heart?

Their son tells them he plans to begin a diet. Doing their best to seem unalarmed, the husband and the wife ask what their son means. He isn't sure, he says, but he wants something that will cleanse him. This is the word he uses, and it sounds funny, the wife will later say, coming from a boy his age. They tell him that a focus on diet is a good idea, but that he needs to remember that diet is a word that means everything we eat and that every diet should include nutritious foods.

They tell him to be careful to get sufficient calories. They hear themselves lecturing and try to stop, but it's too late. Though he's still in the room, their son is no longer listening to them. Later, both husband and wife will feel guilty about their reaction. We should have heard him out, the husband says. The wife nods her head but says nothing.

Their daughters giggle in the kitchen. When they come to investigate, the husband and the wife find the girls pointing out the window. When they ask what has inspired such delight, their daughters point at the fat man running by again and say they're having a great time imagining what he does for work. One says that the fat man is an elephant trainer. Another says he drives a steamroller or maybe he's a hot-air balloonist. Another says he's an elevator operator. They roar at this and stand up to mime what it must be like to share an elevator with this enormous man. They imagine the way he looks in his ill-fitting uniform, gold buttons bursting, a tiny hat teetering on his too-large head. The fat man can't know what the daughters have said about him, but it bothers the wife all the same. What bothers her more, she says, is the way the girls so casually abused this man right in front of her, how entirely comfortable they were belittling a man while she and their father were in the room. Ease up, says the husband. We would have acted that way once. We would have done the same thing. No, says the wife, not me.

On television there's a documentary about paragliders, these men and women flying on parachutes. They see them and are amazed. They have no propulsion, no engine to help them gain altitude, and still, even though they should be falling, they find ways to climb and stay aloft. The narrator explains that these paragliders find ridge lift, gaining altitude on currents that come up and over outcroppings of rock. The best paragliders, she says, know how to find thermals, pockets of warm air created when the sun heats the earth. She says that a good glider will ride a thermal for hours. Doesn't it seem strange? says the husband. Doesn't it seem, in the age of airplanes and satellites, a little old-fashioned? The wife says that she can't help but wonder what it feels like to rise up in a column of warm air, to be lighter than the forces around her, to have a kind of negative weight that will not be pulled to the earth.

Their daughters are changing. They have watched them as they seem to be discovering their bodies, wearing clothing that accentuates their femininity and their burgeoning adulthood: their shoulders bare, their stomachs too often exposed. The husband and the wife have gathered up the fashion magazines and makeup and piles of clutter their daughters leave everywhere. A couple of years ago, it was all secret clubhouse meetings and whispers between girlfriends. Now they hear talk of parties and who will be there and whether parents are in or out of town. It's probably time, the husband says, to return to the topics of alcohol and drugs, boys and sex. It's time for follow-up conversations, he says. We were their friends before, and maybe their confidantes, but we need to be firmer now. Not advice from friends, but rules from authority figures. He feels confident, he says, that the girls will benefit from a little heart-to-heart. Absolutely, the wife says. It's the right idea, but why doesn't he leave it to her? She'll pull them aside at the right moment. She'll ask how things are at school and with their friends. She'll ask the right questions, mother to daughter. Okay, says the husband, his hands up defensively. Fine.

The fat man runs so slowly that the husband hesitates to even call it by that name. It is running, though, he assures the wife, because there are moments between steps when both his feet are off the ground. Is that right? the wife says.

Is that the definition of running? Yes, says the husband. How do you know that? says the wife. How did you come to that definition? The husband doesn't know why he knows it or where he learned it, but he's certain of it, that walking requires one foot or the other to be in contact with the ground at any given moment. It's fascinating, the wife says. I never would have thought through it myself. Well, says the husband, there has to be some distinction, doesn't there? I guess, says the wife. The husband keeps his eyes on the fat man and moves his head up and down slightly, following the movement as though counting steps. If you think about it, he says, running is like a series of battles with gravity. We push up and gravity pushes down, we push up and it pushes down, over and over and over again. The husband cranes his neck to follow the fat man up the street. He keeps bobbing his head up and down, up and down in a perfectly rhythmic pattern.

The earth science book on the kitchen table belongs to their son. It's open to a chapter on light and heat, and the wife sees that her son has underlined information about thermal convection. Look, she says to the husband, look at this. As he reads, she says that they should tell their son about paragliding and give him a chance to tell them what he knows, to put his knowledge to use. She suspects, she says, that he might feel what she felt at his age, that too little of what he studies is necessary in real life. She says she wonders how the next years will change their son. Who knows, says the husband.

The strong men on television lift enormous stone spheres, moving them from one place to another. They can hardly get their enormous arms around the things. The commentators say that each sphere weighs close to 300 pounds and that most people would find it impossible to even roll one of them more than a few feet. The commentators say that these men are practiced and cautious in their lifting techniques and that no one should attempt this at home. You'll need a good chiropractor, they say. The commentators laugh and the strong men turn red in the face, and the wife says she thinks the guy in the blue tank top is probably going to win. The husband says, Hey champ, and the wife turns to see that their son has entered the room. He stands there and looks at the television like he's deciding whether or not to join them. The husband asks him to pull up a chair and see how amazing these strong men are, but the son just stands there. When the husband offers his own chair, the son says, No, thanks. He has homework.

They watch a show about trains and the host explains just how massive a locomotive engine really is. To demonstrate he takes a coin and places it on the tracks. After the train has passed the coin is still there, now wafer-thin. The host says that people shouldn't try what he's just demonstrated because it can cause major problems. Besides, what good is a flattened coin? The husband mentions to the wife that their son collects coins, or used to anyway, and that he must have it stashed away somewhere. It's been a few years, he says. Must be a small fortune, he says. Yes, the wife says, probably is.

The husband watches the fat man running and wonders out loud what will give first: his will or his body. This can't go on, he says. He'll have to see the futility of it before too long. He says that he imagines that the fat man's doctor told him to lose some weight. He wants to tell the fat man to go back to whatever it was he was doing before he became this carnival attraction on their street. He wants to tell him that he's doing more harm than good. He wants to tell him what he's heard: that too much of anything is bad for you, even if that thing is wholesome and good, even if that thing is something you love, something that makes you happy. He wants to tell the fat man that too much fiber will strain the digestive tracts, or that citric acid erodes tooth enamel, or that it's possible, can you believe it, to die from drinking too much water. He wants to tell him about the damage he's doing to his knees. He wants to tell him what his daughters have been saying. He wants to tell him to stop it already, to go home, to quit, to give it up. The husband turns to his wife, but she isn't there. He calls for her, saying that she should come and see what he's seeing. When the wife doesn't reply, the husband calls again. The husband waits for his wife and then he turns to watch the fat man, but the fat man is gone and the street empty.

Undone by the Moon

Mr. *Dall hasn't slept* through the night in years, and he blames it on his testicles. He can't remember the last time he slept for more than three consecutive hours, and he doesn't even answer when his wife asks, first thing each morning, whether he was up in the night. He just waves her off. It's not actually the testicles that keep him awake. It's the drugs, a messy cocktail of things meant to keep him alive, but there might be more to it. He sometimes thinks he's being punished. Because there are nights when it's not the pain keeping him up. He thinks someone might be there, just outside the window, delighting in his discomfort.

Mrs. Glass says that the barking has got to stop and that owners should have the decency to shut their beasts up. It's common courtesy. She says it's bad enough that she should have to watch her step on the sidewalks, but this barking, night after night, is too much. Mrs. Lassiter is proud to announce that the barking annoys her as well and that she's glad it isn't coming from her house. Not mine, she says, you can be sure of that. Mrs. Glass doesn't really care which dogs are barking and which are not. She feels certain, though, that things around here would improve if a few of these dogs were to go missing. Mrs. Lassiter says that Mrs. Glass should hold it right there, that maybe she should think about what she's saying because it sounds like she's bargaining for a heap of trouble. Mrs. Glass says that she's not saying anything, that she simply needs some decent sleep. Still, in her bed at night, Mrs. Glass grows uneasy when all the dogs stop barking at once.

Mr. Ramsey knows he's not the only one moving through his house in the long middle of the night. He has company, he says, as he wanders through his living room or den, or into the guest bedroom too cluttered for a guest. He hasn't seen the man who wanders with him, the ghost who keeps breaking things. Mr. Ramsey has tried to communicate, saying loudly into the darkness that the ghost should make himself comfortable. He's asked the ghost if he once lived here, if there's some unfinished business keeping him from his final rest. Those efforts to communicate have begun to taper. In fact, the only thing he says anymore when he and his silent companion wander together is that he wishes the ghost could be a little less clumsy. Would it kill you? he asks loudly. In the mornings, when his wife mumbles complaints about the volume of late-night television, Mr. Ramsey says he's sorry, that he'll try to keep it down.

Mrs. Glenn says to Mr. Glenn that she doesn't know what to say to the children anymore. She's tried and tried to answer their questions, but they're determined to know more than she can tell them. All their questions, she says, are about death and hell and the afterlife, and she wants to reassure them that heaven is available to everyone and that they need not worry about eternal punishments if they live the way they should, but chapters and verses do little to quell their fears. And it *is* fear, she says, not just time wasting. She's seen that behavior and knows how to handle it. These children seem genuinely concerned when they ask her whether they should believe in hauntings and poltergeists. When she asks the children to explain their motivations, to explain why they have taken such an active interest in the church's doctrines regarding death and the beyond, they simply shrug and say it's just something they've been thinking about. Mr. Glenn doesn't know what to say. It's a real dilemma. He wishes his wife could just relax, let it go, get some shut-eye. Mrs. Glenn can't decide if she should calm the children and ease their worry, or if she should tell them what she knows, that their fear can't begin to compete with hers.

Mr. Caldwell is staring out his kitchen window at three in the morning, wondering again why on earth he has such trouble staying asleep. This is the fourth time since ten o'clock last night he's found himself not only awake but up, out of bed, worrying about the exhaustion he'll feel in the morning. He's staring at thick, rounded drops of paint that have dried on the outside of his kitchen window, wondering if a razor blade will do the trick, wondering how he could have missed so much in cleanup, wondering if the color is really one he can live with. He's staring at the fruit tree growing in Mr. Volz's yard, how it rises ten feet before it spreads and hangs over the fence separating one yard from another, thinking about the strange little plums it will drop in a few weeks, how they'll fall all at once, and how so many will rot there in his grass, overripe and waiting for the dogs to find them, roll in them, bring that awful smell into the house. He's staring out his window, holding a glass of water, thinking about finally scheduling a sleep study, a night of electrodes and questionnaires. He's staring past his yard and past Mr. Volz's yard, seeing the raised flower bed Mrs. Hastings is so proud of. He wonders how much time she's spent on that thing, how many weekends she's knelt there in the dirt, digging and planting and pruning. He remembers the night he saw her gardening at two a.m., working by a mechanic's light hung from a low branch. When he saw her the next day, he asked how the late-night gardening was coming along. She didn't answer. She just walked away as quickly as she could.

Mr. Evans is in the middle of a standoff. He can't bear the heat, but he'll be damned if he's going to run the air conditioning through the night. Thirty minutes, he says, that's all any house needs. Just thirty minutes in the middle of the afternoon, before the temperature reaches its peak and before the house has had a chance to become an oven. He opens some windows and doors, closes others, and claims to know just how to force a breeze through the house. The science of keeping cool is all about observation, he says. Mrs. Evans has been trying to break the bank. She waits until he's asleep before she cranks up the cold air, before she starts in on her wasteful ways. And then, Mr. Evans says, and then she has the nerve to plead ignorance. She sits there with her crossword puzzles and claims never to have touched the thermostat, saying again and again that she wouldn't even know which buttons to push. She goes so far, Mr. Evans says, as calling their daughters on the phone and complaining about the forgetfulness of their father, the rantings of a miser. She manages to have these conversations just as he's walking through the kitchen or bedroom, acting as though she were having this conversation anyway and that's it's not on his account. He keeps himself awake at night, both eyes closed, just waiting for his wife to move, to get out of bed and inch toward her designs. He lies there in the heat, his pillow damp with sweat, and waits. But nothing. He might stay awake all night and still, there's no explaining how the heat turned cool, how his wife did it.

Mr. Stewart has rings under his eyes. He says he killed his lawn on purpose. It's all part of a plan to replace the crabgrass with a new, healthier sod. He might even try clover. He says that he thought about simply turning off the water and letting the grass die on its own, but he wanted to get the new grass in before the summer ended. When questioned about the wisdom of his decision, he admits that he really ought to have killed the grass later in the year, when the weather was cooler. He admits that he doesn't really have a plan. When asked what he used to kill the grass so quickly, he stammers and says that it was a weed killer. When informed that weed killers are formulated to kill everything but grass, he finally admits that he used some old thing he found in his garage and claims that he doesn't remember what it was. Maybe it wasn't weed killer, maybe it was something else. Maybe it doesn't matter. Maybe everyone should just stop asking so many questions because he doesn't have the answers they're looking for. Mr. Stewart looks at his pale-brown lawn. He reaches down to touch it, thinks better of the idea, and then turns toward his front door. I can't explain it, he says.

Mrs. Anderson's dentist wants to know if she grinds her teeth when she sleeps. Mrs. Anderson wants to know what her dentist means. What he means, he says, is that the problems with her teeth—the small chips she keeps finding, the sensitivity she's been complaining about—all of it may be the result of grinding. He asks again, does she grind her teeth when she sleeps? No, Mrs. Anderson says, she knows what he means, but she wants to know how one would know such a thing. I mean, she says, if I'm sleeping, how am I to know what my teeth are up to? Well, her dentist says, has your husband reported any grinding? Does the pain seem worse in the morning? Oh, she says, and nods her head like her dentist is finally talking sense. She says, No, there's no grinding that she knows of, but—and she trails off here, staring at the ceiling like she's just seen some awful thing hanging from it. As she stares, her mouth hangs open.

Mrs. Alton tells her son that her dreams have been getting weirder and weirder. Is that a word, she wants to know: weirder? Should she have said more weird? Mrs. Alton can't stop worrying about her grammar whenever she telephones her son. Which is it, she asks, weirder or more weird? Her son asks if she can be more specific about these dreams she's been having. Mrs. Alton tells her son that she's always being chased, that for one reason or another she finds herself the object of pursuit. Like a spy movie, she says. She says that the dreams are doing a number on her nerves. She says that she doesn't wake up anymore unless her heart is pounding and her forehead is covered in sweat. It's weird, she says, isn't it weird? Aren't I too old for those kinds of dreams?

Mr. Hargrove says that this town is shrinking, and he has the aerial photography to prove it. Look, he says, look at this. He takes a yardstick to a photograph and demonstrates. His neighbors have grown weary of this conversation and have grown impatient with the aggression of Mr. Hargrove's claims. Give it up, they say, just let it go. Mr. Hargrove, sometimes red in the face, sometimes relaxed, but always speaking too quickly and too loudly, says that there's no time to waste. He says that the borders of this town are moving and that it won't be long before the entire place simply collapses on itself. It may seem slow, he admits, it may seem like this movement is glacial and therefore not to be worried about, but the rate is increasing, and the effects will most surely be felt in a matter of a few short years. We must hurry, he says, we must find a means of reversing the forces that will compress our homes and the homes of our loved ones. Those who will engage Mr. Hargrove are likely to argue that the borders in question, the ones Mr. Hargrove is comparing in his photographs, are municipal borders and that this is a legal question. Take it to City Hall, they say. No, Mr. Hargrove says, no, you don't understand. Through the night, Mr. Hargrove slouches over his drafting table measuring the distance between physical landmarks on maps of his own making.

Mr. Clifton knows there's asbestos lining the ceiling of his house. He knows there's lead paint in every room. He knows that the wiring inside his walls is covered by only the thinnest layer of plastic. He knows that the tree house in his backyard is not as secure as it ought to be, relying too much on the strength of one branch, a branch no thicker than his own arm. He knows that children can die in their sleep for no reason at all. He knows there are impurities in his water. He knows his job is only as secure as the various fortunes of his industry, an industry that has encountered setback after setback, and that is due to collapse at any moment. He knows his retirement depends on his continued employment, as do his children's college funds. He knows his wife discovered something in her breast that might be a lump and might be nothing. He knows a cycle of sleeplessness and exhaustion. He knows exactly how late it is. He knows his fears are justified.

The Funambulist

There *was a man in our town* who walked everywhere. We saw him making his way up and down our streets at all hours of the day. We saw him walking so often that we wondered when he ever stopped. He was a pleasant man and would wave if we honked or shouted, but he rarely looked at us or seemed concerned by the noises we made. All we knew for sure was that he walked and walked and never seemed to stop even though many of us had seen him doing other things: buying groceries or mailing a letter or paying his utilities. We knew he was probably just an old man without a car, but we loved to talk about the oddity of him. This is, of course, because we knew so little about him. And because we remember so vividly the morning he entered the tallest building in our town, took the stairs to the roof, and walked off it.

The wealthiest bartender in our town says that the man wasn't so old as we like to remember him. He says the man was younger by far than he looked, and it's only our doctors who have made us believe that the man was healthy. Our wealthiest bartender says he lost a great deal of business because of that man, because of the stories about him that began to circulate. He invites us to consider how healthy the man could be if he lived alone and kept his eyes on the ground. He asks us to think about mental health and asks us, please, to consider the value of camaraderie, of enjoying ourselves a little, of a drink.

Our teenagers weren't there the day the man walked into and then off our tallest building, but they know people who were. They have all the details. They know, for example, that the man was wearing sunglasses that morning and that he never had before. They know that he was wearing a green mechanic's jumpsuit. They know that a human body falls down much more quickly than it climbs up. Each of our teenagers claims to have known the man more intimately than their peers. Some of them say they were invited into his house but rejected the offer out of fear or common sense. Some say he lived with his mother who made him do every-thing for her and never left the house. Some say he had more cats than could be counted. Our teenagers call the man crazy and old and say that you can still find remnants of his fall on the sidewalk. They say that parts of his body are all over town or that the old man is not dead, but hiding, waiting for those of us who are foolish enough to leave parties alone.

We remember how cold it was. It was late August and should have been boiling, but the wind came out of nowhere and the temperature plummeted. We shivered for the better part of a week, too stubborn to bundle up. We said we couldn't remember any summer ending so quickly. Though it got warm again just a few days later, we felt we'd been cheated of a season. Something had been taken from us. We felt confused by our inability to see the cold coming or going. What we knew was that a man walked off our tallest building and that the weather changed.

One of the bus drivers in our town has repeatedly asked us to remember the length of wire strung so tightly between our tallest buildings. He's asked us to remember that the man who fell was attempting something other than a fall. We're in no position to question the account of a man who drove past those buildings so many times every day, but we remember no length of wire. If such wire existed, it might be easier to believe that the man had taken a misstep. This is something we would like to believe. We understand mistakes, and we understand desire, but we struggle to understand hopelessness, which is what so many among us have called the old man's fall. If he was attempting something great and missed his mark, we would have no recourse but to praise him. We want to admire the attempt, but we saw no wire.

On the days immediately after the fall we expected to read some account of it in the paper. The writers for our paper are men and women who won't allow us to call them journalists, feeling that journalism is something more than our small town can claim. They didn't write the story we looked for and this is because they couldn't find two accounts that didn't conflict. They interviewed street vendors, vagrants, people who had been on their way to work, anyone who claimed to know anything about what happened. They heard that a man fell, that a man had been shot, that a woman jumped, that a child was thrown, that a family elected a scapegoat, that a circus performer made a mistake, that nothing happened. These accounts, they said, were nothing they could work with, and so they wrote instead of our recent festival, how our children performed folk dances from around the world

Our children sing rhymes about the man who fell. They sing that he was an angel who forgot how to fly. They sing that he was a devil lost in our world. They sing words that we wonder at and words that we've never heard. Our children grow quiet when we ask where they learned such things.

They're shy and removed when we press them for details, saying only that they don't know or that they're sorry.

We've questioned our meteorologists about the weather. They tell us that it's common that we should get a stretch of cold long before the weather turns for good. They have charts to prove it, but we're inclined to disagree. We've lived too many years to believe everything that gets put to paper, and we know that the weather never turned so cold so quickly and for such a short time. We wouldn't have been surprised by snow during that long week. We want to ask our meteorologists to explain how this could be. We want to know if there's something else that might explain the shift. We want them to tell us about a storm that occurs only once in a hundred years, bringing winds from thousands of miles away. We want to hear about floods and droughts. We want to hear about the rising temperature of the ocean. We want to hear about pollutants in our air and soil. We tell them that there must be some larger explanation for such a chill so early in the year. We tell them we're not prepared to accept their charts. They apologize and tell us that they've given us all they can.

There are those among us who claim to have seen a photograph of the man just moments before he fell. Based on the angle, the photograph must have been taken from the second-tallest building in our town. The photograph, they say, is in black and white and catches the man staring forward but with his head bent down at a slight angle. His eyes are not visible and the shape of his body is concealed beneath baggy clothing. The man's face, they say, is covered almost entirely by his beard, but it's easy to see how thin he is. The photograph has circulated, some say, and has been lost among the many hands that touched it. Though many claim knowledge of it, no one seems ready to say where they saw it or who showed it to them. No one claims to have taken the photograph.

Our ambulance drivers have no record of any call to the scene that day. They say that while they heard secondhand accounts, they know of no vehicle sent and no body recovered. Their records do show activity elsewhere that morning, and more of it than usual. A women felt a flutter in her left arm and knew what that meant. A retired general had a stroke. A baby was given food that its mother could never have known it was allergic to. A teenage boy fell at school and bit off a piece of his tongue. A case of pneumonia was caught. A bone was broken. An eye was bruised. A piece of candy got mostly swallowed but stuck somewhere in a throat.

Our teenagers say that as a body falls five stories it makes a sound like the quick rustle of a bird's wings. We know, of course, that our teenagers are bound to be fascinated by death, and especially death by apparent suicide, but we fear their fixation is unhealthy. We tell them that suicide is not necessarily what this is. We remind them that whatever they may see on television or in movies, ours is not a town like others. The things that happen elsewhere rarely happen here. Please, we say, let's not dwell on this one exception.

There are stores in our town that sell nothing unless it's rare and collectible. This is where we were most likely to see the man who fell before he fell. In his absence, we've visited these shops more often. We know little of records, stamps, comics, and model trains, but it's apparent to us now that whole worlds exist to maintain and care for such things. We ask the owners of these stores what they knew of the man who spent so many hours there. In each case the answer is the same: the store owners tell us that the man never bought anything but that he seemed to have other suppliers. He lectured them for hours, they say, about prices and value and the small details that revealed a forgery. He knew a lot, they say, but they grew tired of the man who never bought from them and who made it difficult to address the needs of customers who might.

Our clergy have said little about the man who fell from our tallest building. We've asked them to address the issue, to tell us something that will show things in a different light. Our clergy have said only that the world is a far more mysterious place than we can know. They remind us that they've said all this before. We say that we have a context now and would like to revisit these topics. They're delighted by our interest, they say, and prepare sermons that we're bound to like, but these sermons give us little we can use. They tell us to be kind to each other, to focus our attentions on service. They tell us that goodness is always met with greater goodness. We know these things. These are things we've heard only too many times.

Our doctors say that it's unlikely that a living body could sustain the force of a fall from our tallest building. We've asked them if it were possible that the man who fell didn't die but stood up and walked away. They tell us no. They tell us we're dealing with probabilities so small they're not worth considering. They tell us that after a fall like that, it wouldn't even be worth rushing to the hospital, that it wouldn't make a difference. We ask them about physics. We've heard that a human body, falling from a building, could be sucked in through an open window. Such things have been reported, and we want to know if it's possible. The doctors have no answer for us, but they're willing to hazard that while it may be possible for a body to be sucked into a window it would need, in all likelihood, to be the window of a very tall building. Our tallest building isn't probably tall enough. We're disappointed each time we think of this. We're disappointed to remember that our skyline is hardly something to admire. We're saddened to admit that our doctors are probably right.

Those new to our town ask if it's true that a man once attempted to cross the space between our two tallest buildings on a wire no thicker than a human thumb. They ask if it's true that he was famous for having crossed greater heights than this before. They ask if we can remember the morning, not so long ago, when our streets filled as we watched a man defy gravity. They've heard that the police attempted to stop the man but were too late and were forced to watch, standing at either end of his wire, waiting for him to finish. They say the police intended to arrest the man for disturbing the peace, that such feats were likely to encourage other such feats, and that people would hurt themselves. They say that the man sat on his wire—actually sat there—actually got off his feet and sat on the wire for what seemed days. They say that the crowd below him grew and grew and that there was hardly space to stand. They say that the whole town was amazed and dumbfounded. They say that no one knows what happened to the man, that no one knows how he got off the wire. They ask us if we can fill in the blanks, if we can tell them how things ended. They want us to tell them if the man was arrested or if he was fined. They ask to know all we know, so we tell them. We tell them there was no crowd, no police, no wire.

We've overheard our teenagers telling jokes about the rate at which a body will fall in a vacuum. We've heard them saying that a feather will fall just as fast, and we've heard the disbelief that always follows such observations. We've asked our teenagers to have more respect, to speak less casually about what they don't understand. We've asked them to stop dropping eggs from rooftops.

We find ourselves walking more than ever before. On bright days and when the weather is nice, we wander the streets. We don't say to one another that we're trying to see what we will later wish we had seen. We don't say what it might be we're looking for, but if we're being honest, we are looking for something. Because something's missing. Our town isn't as whole as it once was. When people who are new to town ask if it's true that a man once walked on a wire between our tallest buildings, and if it wasn't the same man they saw on television last night, doing the same thing between skyscrapers somewhere in Japan or Australia, we tell them what we know to be true. No such man ever lived in our town. Our tallest buildings are not so tall.

Aboard Abroad

Problem:

Four people sit in a train compartment in which two seats face two seats. Each person, therefore, sits next to one person, across from another, and at the diagonal from a third. Solve to determine each person's profession, hat color, and country of origin.

Givens:

1. The person sitting neither across from nor directly next to the man wearing the green hat has a PhD in mathematics. His dissertation, a summary of advances in the field of automated deduction, was largely plagiarized from a series of papers his advisor recommended even though he—the advisor—had never read them. His work requires no specialized knowledge or expertise.

2. The woman sitting next to the German is not wearing a green hat or a blue hat or a white hat or a black hat or a yellow hat or a gray hat or a purple hat. She wonders why it's so hot in here.

3. The dentist is not a real dentist, but few people know this. Among the people who do know it is the Cuban, who would not be here if not for that knowledge and all that it represents, if not for the problems associated

with the work the dentist does when not pretending to be a dentist, if not for his crimes, if not for the expectation that she should eliminate the threat embodied by the dentist.

4. The American believes she passes easily for a German. The trick of it, she says, is to adopt an unyielding affection for common products of German manufacture. Toothpaste, for example, and fabric softener. Though in truth, there's no call for the American to feign connection to that country or those people. Her maternal grandmother was German and her mother lived outside Köln during her earliest years, but these facts are of no consequence. She often disdains the behaviors and attitudes she considers unique to her compatriots, and she confesses to her closest friends that it's a snobbery she wishes she could avoid. She sometimes apologizes to her students for her Teutonic thoroughness. They nod or smile but have no idea what she means.

5. The woman wearing the purple hat (who is uncomfortable with a purple hat, believing it makes her conspicuous when she ought to be inconspicuous) has the explicit instruction to find and eliminate the man sitting directly in front of her, knee to knee. The information she was given indicates that the man has no suspicion of her, but the way he stares and refuses to look away makes her wonder if something or someone might have clued him in, tipped him off, spilled the beans.

6. The Serbian isn't a programmer, practically speaking, but something closer to an office manager.

7. The man in the brown hat hates the words currently in vogue related to legal relationships between men who love men and women who love women. Especially in English, and particularly in the United States, where he spends too much of his time. He hates the very

sound of phrases like "domestic partnership" and "civil union." He hates just as much the word "cohabitation." More than these, he feels a literal shiver anytime he hears the word "lover," the way it reduces a person to his or her sexual relationship to another. He hates it no matter how it gets applied, or to whom. It has become his primary example when asked to explain why the English language pales next to his native tongue.

8. The person in the red hat knows nothing of mathematics and nothing of spies and spying and nothing of government secrets sold for personal profit. But she knows a thing or two about cigar smoke and feels only contempt for those who produce it, or as is the case with the man to her left, those who hold unlit cigars in their mouths as though to brag about the awful thing they mean to do just as soon as they find a match or lighter. It's very hot in here. She worries that any moment now the man might light up, making things worse, and she feels a sudden longing for the smoke-free environments that are among the virtues of her homeland. She waves a train timetable at her face, an improvised fan, and wonders if train windows can be opened.

9. The Serbian hates German fabric softeners but doesn't know it. What he knows is that the woman sitting across from him, too close to him, stinks of something chemical and awful.

10. The German smokes a cigar (holds an unlit cigar in his mouth, wishes he were smoking it, longs for a puff) and believes that his life is filled with spectral presences. He wonders if the people sharing this train compartment have physical form or only appear to. He wonders, particularly, about the woman sitting in front of him, how calmly, unflinchingly, patiently she sits there. It's not human, the German thinks, to be

so calm and so unflinching. There's something about her that isn't right. It might be her hat, which matches nothing else about her. Why lavender, the German wonders. Or is it violet? Why does it remind him of the dead and dying?

11. The spy has much in common with the non-dentist. She too pretends to be someone she's not. She too lives under multiple layers of deceit and subterfuge. She's known as many things to many people and worries, constantly, that she might one day lose the sense of order she has worked so hard to maintain. She worries, that is, that she might one day lose the thread of things, that it might all unravel.

12. The person sitting diagonal from the woman wearing the purple hat has a chocolate bar that will not be shared with anyone. The quality of that chocolate is greater than any to be found on the entire North American continent. In North America, the chocolate isn't even chocolate. Its wax made to look like chocolate. It's a cruel joke played on idiots.

13. The non-female, non-spy, non-non-dentist often confuses the phrases "discrete mathematics" and "discreet mathematics." To date, no one has corrected the error. In truth, he knows virtually nothing of mathematics, but because of a quirk in the university policies for naming positions, he's often mistaken for the head of the programming section of the computer engineering department. Too often, he's compelled to explain that he's not the head of programming. He's the head of programs. It would make more sense to call him a chair or a coordinator, but the university insists that those titles are reserved for academic units.

14. The man who is not wearing a brown hat is also not wearing a green hat. Instead, he's holding his green hat, spinning it end over end, running his fingers on

and around its brim, inspecting it, considering it. The hat is a new one, size 21 and 7/8 inches, which is, by most standards, small or medium small. The size of a man's head is no indication of his intelligence, everyone knows that, but the man not wearing a brown hat can't help but wonder if what everyone knows is a reliable guarantee. He wonders if his intelligence is lacking and if the size of his head is a clear indication of that fact. He wonders, too, if the size of his head, irrespective of what it may or may not say about his intelligence, might incline people, such as the people in this train compartment, to assume some deficiency on his part. Do they think I'm slow? he wonders. Do people think me a fool? Does this woman sitting in front of me think I'm an idiot? And why not? What would tell her otherwise?

15. The person sitting across from the person not currently wearing a green hat has not seen her mother in more than six years. They parted, that last time, on polite terms, but she carries the sense that something unfinished between them must, sooner or later, be seen to and accounted for. Her mother, she knows, must wonder where she is and why she doesn't call and why her letters have gone unanswered. The explanation is simple, but the woman sitting across from the person not really wearing a green hat is obligated (professionally, morally) to say nothing, to explain nothing. She carries some guilt for what she's done to her mother even if she's trained herself against demonstrations of that guilt. She knows which questions on which tests are designed to determine whether or not she's the kind of person who might feel and subsequently be swayed by the kind of guilt she carries with her. She's not that kind of person. She refuses to be that kind of

person. But still, at times like these, her resolve seems more brittle than it once was.

16. The programmer speaks six languages and has adopted, as a result, a peculiar accent that leads others, especially strangers he interacts with in the village of his birth, to wonder aloud where he's from. They have wondered, with delighted grins, what brings him here, to this part of the world. They have wondered, based on his accent, if he might not be vacationing from Germany or someplace farther north. Why here, they ask, so far into the hills, so far from the cities?

17. The woman in the red hat would like very much to drift off for a few minutes. She fears, though, that were she to do so, she might sleep right through her stop, which is, she thinks, one of the next two or three. It's hard to say. More importantly, she worries that if she were to slip away for a moment, her head might nod and her hat might fall off, and then where would she be? Because the hat is the sign she gave to the man who promised to meet her, and if she weren't wearing the hat, how in the world would he know that she was she? She couldn't be more sure that without this hat she'd blend in all too easily. When she suggested a red hat, she thought it would be a more distinguishing feature. She never expected to find herself among so many hat-wearing people. Here in this train compartment, for example, 100% of the people are wearing—or at least holding—hats, and not just ordinary brown and black ones (though there is one of those), but also a green one and a purple one, every bit as conspicuous as hers. What if the man should see this other woman, this woman sitting at the diagonal from her, and forget for a moment that it was a red hat he was after? What if that man were to take this other woman by that arm

and traipse off across Europe with that other woman and her purple hat?

18. The Cuban is not and never has been married. The American was engaged once, briefly. The Serbian is not married and sees no reason to expect that to change, given the state of things. The German is twice divorced and has four children, one from his first marriage, two from his second, and one that neither of his wives knows anything about.

19. The German has never been mistaken for anything but a German, but he often wakes at night and feels a strange sense that he isn't at home, that he has, instead, been transported by unfriendly forces to a place that only looks familiar. He fears that these forces have only yet shown him a small portion of their power and that any day now he might wake to discover the full, unmitigated force of so much spite. Despite the heat, the thought gives him a chill. He needs, more than anything, a bit of fresh air. He leans toward the woman on his right and whispers, conspiratorially, that he would like to switch seats with her. Excuse me? the woman says. He looks at the woman as though they both know all too well that she heard him plainly the first time. I'm sorry, she says, with a hint of panic in her voice, but no. The German shrugs and stands. At the very least, he says, perhaps I could ask you to watch my hat for a moment. He passes through the compartment door and into the main corridor of the train. His hat remains in his now empty seat.

20. The Cuban waits exactly twenty seconds and then follows the German, leaving in the train compartment the programmer, the head of programs, and a green hat.

Acknowledgments

My thanks to the editors of the journals where the following stories first appeared:

Hayden's Ferry Review: "Amanuensis"

Ninth Letter: "Keepers of Bees"

Gettysburg Review: "Rosenvall's Cage"

Western Humanities Review: "Age, Era, Epoch, Eon"

The Colorado Review: "The Trees in North America"

Joyland: "At the Gates of the Kingdom"

Black Warrior Review: "The Two Mr. Greens"

The Helicon West Anthology: "The Scold"

The Laurel Review: "Blight"

Hunger Mountain: "The Tree of the Holy Virgin"

Juked: "The Hidden Curriculum"

The Normal School: "In California"

Irreantum: "Maybe the Kids Maybe"

Indiana Review: "The Weather Here"

Sou'wester: "Undone by the Moon"

Crazyhorse: "The Funambulist"

Diagram: "Aboard Abroad"

*   *   *

This book has been a long time in the making, and I'm indebted to many, many friends, teachers, and colleagues who have helped and encouraged me over the years.

I'm grateful to Dr. Ross Tangedal and the incredible staff at Cornerstone Press for the care and attention they've given to my work, to Paige Biever and Lilly Kulbeck for their wise editorial guidance, and to Allison Lange, Sam Bjork, and Sophie McPherson for help with finishing touches.

Thank you to the friends who helped me to improve early drafts: Lance Larsen, Spencer Hyde, Kate Finlinson, and Adrian Thayn. Thank you to David McGlynn, Lynn Kilpatrick, Matthew Batt, Nicole Walker, and Margot Singer for many years of friendship and encouragement. Thank you to Aimee Bender for being a champion of my work when I needed it most. Thank you to François Camoin, Karen Brennan, David Kranes, Kate Coles, and Robin Hemley, for teaching me that there's so much more to writing than writing. Thank you to Melanie Rae Thon for each of our many walks, for invigorating conversation, and for being a constant mentor and friend. Thank you to Erik DeWaal for sticking with me over the decades.

Thank you to my parents for their unceasing support and for sharing with me so many of their own stories. They will know exactly how much I've invented and how much I've borrowed. And to my sons, Henry and Benjamin, for showing me that the world is bursting with great art and bursting with portmanteaus.

Finally, and most importantly, my thanks and my love to Janell, the best travel companion I could ever hope for, the best part of my life.

Stephen Tuttle is a fiction writer and poet. His writing has appeared in *The Nation, The Southern Review, Ploughshares, The Gettysburg Review, The Threepenny Review*, and other venues. He lives with his wife and two dogs in Provo, Utah, and teaches at Brigham Young University.